W9-DIE-462

~

Alanna shrugged. "I think we were talking about what makes a bully."

"A bully fights people littler and weaker than he is because he thinks it's fun," Jonathan said flatly. "Did you enjoy fighting Ralon? We'll forget for now he's older than you and a squire."

"When we were actually *fighting*—maybe," she replied slowly. "After—no."

"You won't find anyone smaller than you are, so you can't beat on them," the older boy said practically. "And after today we're all going to think twice about whether you're the weakest. Look, young Trebond—what did you think studying to be a knight was about?"

Suddenly, Alanna felt much better. "Thanks, Highness." She grinned. "Thanks a lot."

He put a hand on her shoulder. "You may have noticed my friends call me Jonathan, or Jon."

Alanna looked up at him, not sure what was going on. "And am *I* your friend, Highness?"

"I do believe you are," he told her quietly. "I'd like you to be." He offered her his hand.

She took it. "Then I am—Jonathan."

Song of the Lioness Quartet
by Tamora Pierce

Alanna: The First Adventure (Book One)

In the Hand of the Goddess (Book Two)

The Woman Who Rides Like a Man (Book Three)

Lioness Rampant (Book Four)

And look for Tamora Pierce's new Tortall series:

THE IMMORTALS

available for the first time in paperback
from Random House Fantasy in May 1997:

Wild Magic (Book One)

Wolf-Speaker (Book Two)

Emperor Mage (Book Three)

Alanna

The First Adventure

Song of the Lioness
Book One

TAMORA PIERCE

Random House 🏠 New York

Library of Congress Catalog Card Number: 83-2595
ISBN: 0-679-80114-6
RL: 5.7

Printed in the United States of America 16 15 14 13 12

To Claire, who made it all finally happen,
and to Frances, who told me to talk to Claire

Contents

Alanna

The First Adventure

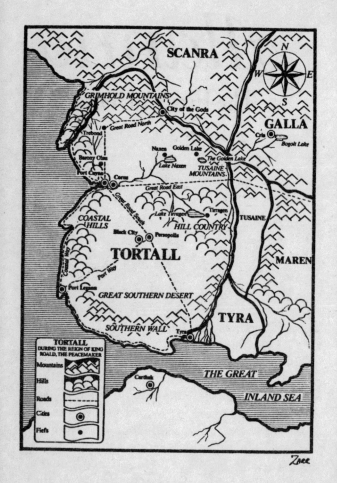

one

Twins

"*That* is my decision. We need not discuss it," said the man at the desk. He was already looking at a book. His two children left the room, closing the door behind them.

"He doesn't want us around," the boy muttered. "He doesn't care what *we* want."

"We *know* that," was the girl's answer. "He doesn't care about anything, except his books and scrolls."

The boy hit the wall. "I don't *want* to be a knight! I want to be a great sorcerer! I want to slay demons and walk with the gods—"

"D'you think I want to be a lady?" his sister asked. "'Walk slowly, Alanna,'" she said primly. "'Sit still, Alanna. Shoulders back, Alanna.' As if that's all I can do with myself!" She paced the floor. "There has to be another way."

The boy watched the girl. Thom and Alanna of Trebond were twins, both with red hair and purple eyes. The only difference between them—as far as most people could tell—was the length of their hair. In face and body shape, dressed alike, they would have looked alike.

"Face it," Thom told Alanna. "Tomorrow *you* leave for the convent, and *I* go to the palace. That's it."

"Why do you get all the fun?" she complained. "I'll have to learn sewing and dancing. You'll study tilting, fencing—"

"D'you think I *like* that stuff?" he yelled. "I *hate* falling down and whacking at things! *You're* the one who likes it, not me!"

She grinned. "*You* should've been Alanna. They always teach the girls magic—" The thought hit her so suddenly that she gasped. "Thom. That's it!"

From the look on her face, Thom knew his sister had just come up with yet another crazy idea. "*What's* it?" he asked suspiciously.

Alanna looked around and checked the hall for servants. "Tomorrow he gives us the letters for the man who trains the pages and the people at the convent. You can imitate his writing, so you can do new letters, saying we're twin boys. *You* go to the convent. Say in the letter that you're to be a sorcerer. The Daughters of the Goddess are the ones who train young boys in magic, remember? When you're older, they'll send you to the priests. And I'll go to the palace and learn to be a knight!"

"That's crazy," Thom argued. "What about your hair? You can't go swimming naked, either. And you'll turn into a girl—you know, with a chest and everything."

"I'll cut my hair," she replied. "And—well, I'll handle the rest when it happens."

"What about Coram and Maude? They'll be traveling with us, and they can tell us apart. They know we aren't twin boys."

She chewed her thumb, thinking this over. "I'll tell Coram we'll work magic on him if he says anything," she said at last. "He hates magic—that ought to be enough. And maybe we can talk to Maude."

Thom considered it, looking at his hands. "You think we could?" he whispered.

Alanna looked at her twin's hopeful face. Part of her wanted to stop this before it got out of hand, but not a very big part. "If you don't lose your nerve," she told her twin. *And if I don't lose mine,* she thought.

"What about Father?" He was already looking into the distance, seeing the City of the Gods.

Alanna shook her head. "He'll forget us, once we're gone." She eyed Thom. "D'you want to be a sorcerer bad enough?" she demanded. "It means years of studying and work for us both. Will you have the guts for it?"

Thom straightened his tunic. His eyes were cold. "Just show me the way!"

Alanna nodded. "Let's go find Maude."

∾

*M*aude, the village healer, listened to them and said nothing. When Alanna finished, the woman turned and stared out the door for long minutes. Finally she looked at the twins again.

They didn't know it, but Maude was in difficulty. She had taught them all the magic she possessed. They were both capable of learning much more, but there were no other teachers at Trebond. Thom wanted everything he could get from his magic, but he disliked people. He listened to Maude only because he thought she had something left to teach him; he hated Coram—the other adult who looked after the twins—because Coram made him feel stupid. The only person in the world Thom loved, beside himself, was Alanna. Maude thought about Alanna and sighed. The girl was very different from her brother. Alanna was afraid of her magic. Thom had to be ordered to hunt, and Alanna had to be tricked and begged into trying spells.

The woman had been looking forward to the day when someone else would have to handle these two. Now it seemed the gods were going to test her through them one last time.

She shook her head. "I cannot make such a decision without help. I must try and See, in the fire."

Thom frowned. "I thought you couldn't. I thought you could only heal."

Maude wiped sweat from her face. She was afraid. "Never mind what I can do and what I cannot do," she snapped. "Alanna, bring wood. Thom, vervain."

They rushed to do as she said, Alanna returning first to add wood to the fire already burning on the hearth. Thom soon followed, carrying leaves from the magic plant vervain.

Maude knelt before the hearth and motioned for the twins to sit on either side of her. She felt sweat running down her back. People who tried to use magic the gods had not given them often died in ugly ways. Maude gave a silent prayer to the Great Mother Goddess, promising good behavior for the rest of her days if only the Goddess would keep her in one piece through this.

She tossed the leaves onto the fire, her lips moving silently with the sacred words. Power from her and from the twins slowly filled the fire. The flames turned green from Maude's sorcery and purple for the twins'. The woman drew a deep breath and grabbed the twins' left hands, thrusting them into the fire. Power shot up their arms. Thom yelped and wriggled with the pain of the magic now filling him up. Alanna bit her lower lip till it bled, fighting the pain her own way. Maude's eyes were wide and blank as she kept their intertwined hands in the flames.

Suddenly Alanna frowned. A picture was forming in the fire. That was impossible—*she* wasn't supposed to See anything. Maude was the one who had cast the spell. Maude was the only one who should See anything.

Ignoring all the laws of magic Alanna had been taught, the picture grew and spread. It was a city made all of black, shiny stone. Alanna leaned forward, squinting to see it better. She had never seen anything like this city. The sun beat down on gleaming walls and towers. Alanna was afraid—more afraid than she had ever been...

Maude let go of the twins. The picture vanished. Alanna was cold now, and very confused. What had that city been? Where was it?

Thom examined his hand. There were no burn marks, or even scars. There was nothing to show that Maude had kept their hands in the flames for long minutes.

Maude rocked back on her heels. She looked old and tired. "I have seen many things I do not understand," she whispered finally. "Many things—"

"Did you see the city?" Alanna wanted to know.

Maude looked at her sharply. "I saw no city."

Thom leaned forward. "*You* saw something?" His voice was eager. "But Maude cast the spell—"

"No!" Alanna snapped. "I didn't see anything! Anything!"

Thom decided to wait and ask her later, when she didn't look so scared. He turned to Maude. "Well?" he demanded.

The healing woman sighed. "Very well. Tomorrow Thom and I go to the City of the Gods."

～

*A*t dawn the next day, Lord Alan gave each of his children a sealed letter and his blessing before instructing Coram and Maude. Coram still did not know the change in plan. Alanna did not intend to enlighten him until they were far from Trebond.

Once Lord Alan let them go, Maude took the twins to Alanna's room while Coram got the horses ready. The letters were quickly opened and read.

Lord Alan entrusted his son to the care of Duke Gareth of Naxen and his daughter to the First Daughter of the convent. Sums of money would be sent quarterly to pay for his children's upkeep until such time as their teachers saw fit to return them to their home. He was busy with his studies and trusted the judgment of the Duke and the First Daughter in all matters. He was in their debt, Lord Alan of Trebond.

Many such letters went to the convent and to the palace every year. All girls from noble families studied in convents until they were fifteen or sixteen, at which time they went to Court to find husbands. Usually the oldest son of a noble family learned the skills and duties of a knight at the King's palace. Younger sons could follow their brothers to the palace, or they could go first to the convent, then to the priests' cloisters, where they studied religion or sorcery.

Thom was expert at forging his father's handwriting. He wrote two new letters, one for "Alan," one for himself. Alanna read them carefully, relieved to see that there was no way to tell the difference between Thom's work and the real thing. The boy sat back with a grin, knowing it might be years before the confusion was resolved.

While Thom climbed into a riding skirt, Maude took Alanna into the dressing room. The girl changed into shirt, breeches and boots. Then Maude cut her hair.

"I've something to say to you," Maude said as the first lock fell to the floor.

"What?" Alanna asked nervously.

"You've a gift for healing." The shears worked on. "It's greater than mine, greater than any I have ever known. And you've other magic, power you'll learn to use. But the healing—that's the important thing. I had a dream last night. A warning, it was, as plain as if the gods shouted in my ear."

Alanna, picturing this, stifled a giggle.

"It don't do to laugh at the gods," Maude told her sternly. "Though you'll find that out yourself, soon enough."

"What is that supposed to mean?"

"Never mind. Listen. Have you thought of the lives you'll take when you go off performing those great deeds?"

Alanna bit her lip. "No," she admitted.

"I didn't think so. You see only the glory. But there's lives taken and families without fathers and sorrow. Think before you fight. Think on who you're fighting, if only because one day you must meet your match. And if you want to pay for those lives you do take, use your healing magic. Use it all you can, or you won't cleanse your soul of death for centuries. It's harder to heal than it is to kill. The Mother knows why, but you've a gift for both." Quickly she brushed Alanna's cropped hair. "Keep your hood up for a bit, but you look enough like Thom to fool anyone but Coram."

Alanna stared at herself in the mirror. Her twin stared back, violet eyes wide in his pale face. Grinning, she wrapped herself in her cloak. With a last peek at the boy in the mirror, she followed Maude out to the courtyard. Coram and Thom, already mounted up, waited for them. Thom rearranged his skirts and gave his sister a wink.

Maude stopped Alanna as she went to mount the pony, Chubby. "Heal, child," the woman advised. "Heal all you can, or you'll pay for it. The gods mean for their gifts to be used."

Alanna swung herself into the saddle and patted Chubby with a comforting hand. The pony, sensing that the good twin was on his back, stopped fidgeting. When Thom was riding him, Chubby managed to dump him.

The twins and the two servants waved farewell to the assembled castle servants, who had come to see them off. Slowly they rode through the castle gate, Alanna doing her best to imitate Thom's pout—or the pout Thom would be wearing if he were riding to the palace right now. Thom was looking down at his pony's ears, keeping his face hidden. Everyone knew how the twins felt at being sent away.

The road leading from the castle plunged into heavily overgrown and rocky country. For the next day or so they would be riding through the unfriendly forests of the Grimhold Mountains, the great natural border between Tortall and Scanra. It was familiar land to the twins. While it might seem dark and unfriendly to people from the South, to Alanna and Thom it would always be home.

At midmorning they came to the meeting of Trebond Way and the Great Road. Patrolled by the King's men, the Great Road led north to the distant City of the Gods. That was the way Thom and Maude would take. Alanna and Coram were bound south, to the capital city of Corus, and the royal palace.

The two servants went apart to say goodbye and give the twins some privacy. Like Thom and Alanna, it would be years before Coram and Maude saw each other again. Though Maude would return to Trebond, Coram was to remain with Alanna, acting as her manservant during her years at the palace.

Alanna looked at her brother and gave a little smile. "Here we are," she said.

"I wish I could say 'have fun,'" Thom said frankly, "but I can't see how anyone can have fun learning to be a knight. Good luck, though. If we're caught, we'll both be skinned."

"No one's going to catch us, brother." She reached across the distance between them, and they gripped hands warmly. "Good luck, Thom. Watch your back."

"There are a lot of tests ahead for you," Thom said earnestly. "Watch *your* back."

"I'll pass the tests," Alanna said. She knew they were brave words, almost foolhardy, but Thom looked as if he needed to hear them. They turned their ponies then and rejoined the adults.

"Let's go," Alanna growled to Coram.

Maude and Thom took the left fork of the Great Road and Alanna and Coram bore right. Alanna halted suddenly, turning around to watch her brother ride off. She blinked the burning feeling from her eyes, but she couldn't ease the tight feeling in her throat. Something told her Thom would be very different when she saw him again. With a sigh she turned Chubby back toward the capital city.

Coram made a face and urged his big gelding forward. He would have preferred doing anything to escorting a finicky boy to the palace. Once he had been the hardiest soldier in the King's armies. Now he was going to be a joke. People would see that Thom was no warrior, and they would blame Coram—the man who was to have taught him the basics of the warrior's craft. He rode for hours without a word, thinking his own gloomy thoughts, too depressed to notice that Thom, who usually complained after an hour's ride, was silent as well.

Coram had been trained as a blacksmith, but

he had once been one of the best of the King's foot soldiers, until he had returned home to Trebond Castle and become sergeant-at-arms there. Now he wanted to be with the King's soldiers again, but not if they were going to laugh at him because he had a weakling for a master. Why couldn't Alanna have been the boy? *She* was a fighter. Coram had taught her at first because to teach one twin was to teach the other, poor motherless things. Then he began to enjoy teaching her. She learned quickly and well— better than her brother. With all his heart Coram Smythesson wished now, as he had in the past, that Alanna were the boy.

He was about to get his wish, in a left-handed way. The sun was glinting from directly overhead— time for the noon meal. Coram grunted orders to the cloaked child, and they both dismounted in a clearing beside the road. Pulling bread and cheese from a saddlebag, he broke off a share and handed it over. He also took the wineskin down from his saddle horn.

"We'll make the wayhouse by dark, if not before," he rumbled. "Till then, we make do with this."

Alanna removed her heavy cloak. "This is fine with me."

Coram choked, spraying a mouthful of liquid all over the road. Alanna had to clap him on the back before he caught his breath again.

"Brandy?" he whispered, looking at the wineskin. He returned to his immediate problem. "By the Black God!" he roared, turning spotty purple. "We're goin' back this instant, and I'm tannin' yer hide for ye when we get home! Where's that devils'-spawn brother of yours?"

"Coram, calm down," she said. "Have a drink."

"I don't want a drink," he snarled. "I want t' beat the two of ye till yer skins won't hold water!" He took a deep gulp from the wineskin.

"Thom's on his way to the City of the Gods with Maude," Alanna explained. "She thinks we're doing the right thing."

Coram swore under his breath. "That witch *would* agree with you two sorcerers. And what does yer father say?"

"Why should he ever know?" Alanna asked. "Coram, you know Thom doesn't want to be a knight. I do."

"I don't care if the two of ye want t' be dancing bears!" Coram told her, taking another swallow from the skin. "Ye're a girl."

"Who's to know?" She bent forward, her small face intent. "From now on I'm Alan of Trebond, the younger twin. I'll be a knight—Thom'll be a sorcerer. It'll happen. Maude saw it for us in the fire."

Coram made the Sign against evil with his right hand. Magic made him nervous. Maude made him nervous. He drank again to settle his nerves. "Lass, it's a noble thought, a warrior's thought, but it'll never work. If ye're not caught when ye bathe, ye'll be turning into a woman—"

"I can hide all that—with your help. If I can't, I'll disappear."

"Yer father will have my hide!"

She made a face. "Father doesn't care about anything but his scrolls." She drew a breath. "Coram, I'm being nice. Thom wouldn't be this nice. D'you want to see things that aren't there for the next ten years? I can work that, you know. Remember when Cook was going to tell Father who ate the cherry tarts? Or the time Godmother tried to get Father to marry her?"

Coram turned pale. The afternoon the tarts were discovered missing, Cook started to see large, hungry lions following him around the kitchens. Lord Alan never heard about the missing tarts. When the twins' godmother came to Trebond to snare Lord Alan as her next husband, she had fled after only three days, claiming the castle was haunted.

"Ye wouldn't," Coram whispered. He had always suspected that the twins had been behind Cook's hallucinations and Lady Catherine's ghosts, but he had kept those thoughts to himself. Cook gave himself airs, and Lady Catherine was cruel to her servants.

Seeing she had struck a nerve, Alanna changed tactics. "Thom can't shoot for beans, and I can. Thom wouldn't be a credit to you. I will, I think.

You said yourself a grown man can't skin a rabbit faster'n me." She fed her last piece of bread to Chubby and looked at Coram with huge, pleading eyes. "Let's ride on. If you feel the same in the morning, we can turn back." She crossed her fingers as she lied. She had no intention of returning to Trebond. "Just don't rush. Father won't know till it's too late."

Coram swigged again from the skin, getting up shakily. He mounted, watching the girl. They rode silently while Coram thought, and drank.

The threat about making him see things didn't worry him much. Instead he thought of Thom's performance in archery—it was enough to make a soldier cry. Alanna was much quicker than her brother. She rarely tired, even hiking over rough country. She had a feel for the fighting arts, and that was something that never could be learned. She was also as stubborn as a mule.

Because he was absorbed in his thoughts, Coram never saw the wood snake glide across the road. Alanna—and Coram's horse—spotted the slithery creature in the same second. The big gelding reared, almost throwing his master. Chubby stopped dead in the road, surprised by these antics. Coram yelled and fought to hold on as his mount bucked frantically, terrified by the snake. Alanna never stopped to think. She threw herself from Chubby's saddle and grabbed for Coram's reins with both hands. Dodging the gelding's flying hooves frantically, she used all her strength and weight to pull the horse down before Coram fell and broke his neck.

The gelding, more surprised than anything else by the new weight on his reins, dropped to all fours. He trembled as Alanna stroked his nose, whispering comforting words. She dug in a pocket and produced an apple for the horse, continuing to pet him until his shaking stopped.

When Alanna looked up, Coram was watching her oddly. She had no way of knowing that he was imagining what Thom would have done in similar circumstances: her twin would have left Coram to fend for himself. Coram knew the kind of courage it took to calm a large, bucking horse. It was the kind of courage a knight needed in plenty. Even so, Alanna was a girl….

By the time they arrived at the wayhouse, Coram was very drunk. The innkeeper helped him to bed while his wife fussed over "the poor wee lad." In her bed that night, Alanna listened to Coram's snores with a wide grin on her lips. Maude had managed to fill the wineskin with Lord Alan's best brandy, hoping her old friend might be more open to reason if his joints were well oiled.

Coram awoke the next morning with the worst hangover he had ever had. He moaned as Alanna entered his room.

"Don't walk so loud," he begged.

Alanna handed him a steaming mug. "Drink.

Maude says this makes you feel better every time."

The man drank deeply, gasping as the hot liquid burned down his throat. But in the end, he *did* feel better. He swung his feet to the floor, gently rubbing his tender skull. "I need a bath."

Alanna pointed to the bath already waiting in the corner.

Coram glared at her from beneath his eyebrows. "Go order breakfast. I take it I'm to call ye 'Alan' now?"

She yelped with joy and skipped from the room.

⚬

*F*our days later they rode into Corus just after dawn. They were part of the stream of people entering the capital for the market day. Coram guided his horse through the crowds, while Alanna tried to keep Chubby close behind him and still see everything. Never in her life had she encountered so many people! She saw merchants, slaves, priests, nobles. She could tell the Bazhir—desert tribesmen—by their heavy white burnooses, just as she spotted seamen by their braided pigtails. She was lucky that Chubby was inclined to stay near Coram's gelding, or she would have been lost in a second.

The marketplace itself was almost more than a girl from a mountain castle could take. Alanna blinked her eyes at the bright colors—piles of orange and yellow fruits, hangings of bright blue and green, ropes of gold and silver chains. Some people were staring as openly as she was. Others shoved their goods under people's noses, shouting for them to buy. Women in tight dresses eyed men from doorways, and children ran underfoot, sneaking their hands into pockets and purses.

Coram missed nothing. "Keep an eye to yer saddlebags," he called back to Alanna. "There are some here as would steal their own mother's teeth!" He seemed to be directing this comment at a tall young man standing near Alanna.

The lean young man grinned, white teeth flashing in his tanned face. "Who, me?" he asked innocently.

Coram snorted and kicked his horse onward. The man winked one bright hazel eye at Alanna and vanished into the crowd. She watched him until someone shouted for her to watch herself. She wondered if he really was a thief. He seemed very nice.

They left the marketplace, taking the Market Way up a long, sloping hill. This led them through districts where rich merchants lived, up past the villas of even richer nobles. The crossing of Market Way and Harmony Way marked the beginning of the Temple District. Here the Market Way changed its name, becoming the Palace Way. Coram straightened his saddle. After his years of soldiering, this was like coming home.

Alanna saw countless temples as they rode through the district. She had heard that a hundred gods were worshiped in Corus. There were enough temples for that many, she thought. She even saw a troop of women dressed in armor, the guard of the Temple of the Great Mother Goddess. These women were armed with great double-headed axes, and they knew how to use them. Their duty was to keep men from ever setting foot on ground sacred to the Great Mother.

Alanna grinned. Someday she would wear armor too, but she wouldn't be confined to temple grounds!

The ground suddenly rose steeply. The Temple District ended here. Above them, crowning the hill, was the royal palace. Alanna looked at it and gasped. Ahead of her was the City Gate, carved with thousands of figures and trimmed with gold. Through this gate in the palace wall, kings and queens came down to the city on holy days. Through this gate the people went to see their rulers on Great Audience Days. The Gate was as high as the wall it pierced: a wall lined with soldiers dressed in the royal gold and red. Behind the wall, level after level of buildings and towers rose, up to the palace itself. The area had its own gardens, wells, stables, barracks and menagerie. Outside the wall on the other side lay the Royal Forest.

All these things Alanna knew from her father's books and maps, but the reality took her breath away as a paragraph written in a book never could.

Coram led the way to the courtyard beside the stables. Here servants awaited the arrival of guests, to show them to their rooms, to guide the arrivals' servants and to take charge of the horses. One such servant approached them.

Coram dismounted. "I'm Coram Smythesson, of Fief Trebond. I'm come with Master Alan of Trebond to begin his service at Court."

The hostler bowed. A royal page rated some respect, but not the respect a full-grown noble would get. "I'll be takin' th' horses, sir," he said, his voice thick with the accent of the city. "Timon!" he called.

A slender young man in royal livery hurried up. "Aye, Stefan?"

"One fer his Grace. I'll see t' the bags."

Alanna dismounted and hugged Chubby for a second, feeling as if he were her last friend. She had to hurry to catch up with Timon and Coram.

"Ye'll show his Grace the proper respect," Coram growled in her ear. "A wizard with a sword, he is, and a better leader ye'll never meet."

Alanna rubbed her nose anxiously. What if something went wrong? What if the Duke guessed?

She glanced at Coram. The man was sweating. Alanna gritted her teeth and thrust her chin forward stubbornly. She would see this through.

two

The New Page

Duke Gareth of Naxen was tall and thin, with dull brown hair that fell into his muddy brown eyes. Though he was plain looking, there was something commanding about him all the same.

"Alan of Trebond, hm?" His voice was thin and nasal. He frowned as he opened the seal on Alanna's letter. "I trust you will do better here than your sire. He was always at his books."

Alanna swallowed hard. The Duke made her nervous. "He still is, sir."

The Duke looked at her sharply, not sure if she was being pert. "Hmph. So I would suppose." He smiled and nodded at Alanna's servingman. "Coram Smythesson. It's been a long time since the Battle of Joyous Forest."

Coram bowed, grinning. "I didn't think yer Lordship'd remember. That was twenty years ago, and me but a lad myself."

"I don't forget it when a man saves my life. Welcome to the palace. You will like it here—though you, boy, will work hard." Duke Gareth turned his attention back to Alanna. "Sit down, both of you." They obeyed. "You're here, Alan of Trebond, to learn what it is to be a knight and a noble of Tortall. It's not easy. You must learn to defend the weak, to obey your overlord, to champion the cause of right. Someday you may even be able to tell what right is." It was impossible to tell if he was joking, and Alanna decided not to ask.

"Until you are fourteen, you will be a page," the Duke went on. "You will wait on table at the evening meal. You will run errands for any lord or lady who asks you. Half your day will be spent learning fighting arts. The other half you will spend with books, in the hope that we can teach you how to think.

"*If* your masters think you are ready, you will be made squire when you are fourteen. Perhaps a knight will choose you as his body squire. If so, you'll tend your master's belongings, run his errands, protect his interests. Your other lessons will continue—they'll be harder, of course.

"When you are eighteen, you'll undergo the Ordeal of Knighthood. If you survive, you will be a Knight of Tortall. Not everyone survives." He held up his left hand, revealing a missing finger. "I lost this in the Chamber of the Ordeal." He sighed.

"Don't worry about the Ordeal now. You have eight years to think about it. For the present, you will live in the pages' wing. Coram rooms with you, but I hope he'll be able to serve the palace guard in his free time."

Coram nodded. "I'd like that, yer Grace."

Duke Gareth smiled thinly. "Excellent. We can use a man of your ability." He looked at Alanna once again. "One of the older pages will sponsor you and show you how things are done. You'll be in his charge until you are familiar with the palace and your duties. If you are obedient and work hard, you won't see me often. Misbehave, and you'll learn how harsh I can be. When you prove yourself worthy, you will be granted free time to go into the city. And make no mistake—you'll earn every privilege you get three times over. You are here to learn chivalry, not to have a good time. Timon"—Alanna realized the servingman had been in the room all along—"take them to their room. Make sure the boy is properly clothed. Also, a guardsman's uniform for Master Smythesson." The Duke measured Alanna with his eyes. "I expect you to begin serving at dinner in five days. You'll wait on me. Have you any questions?"

It took all her strength to say, "No, your Lordship."

"A duke is called 'your Grace.'" The older man smiled and held his right hand out to her. "It is a hard life, but you'll get used to it."

Alanna kissed his hand timidly. "Yes, your Grace." She and the two men bowed and left the Duke's presence.

The pages' wing stretched along the west side of the palace, standing near the walls that overlooked the city. Here Timon showed Alanna and Coram two small rooms, where they would live during Alanna's time as a page. Someone had already placed their baggage inside the door.

Their next stop was with the palace tailors. Realizing they would measure her for her page's uniform, Alanna felt sick. Her mind whirled with visions of being forced to strip, of being caught and sent home in disgrace before she had even had a chance to start.

Instead a scowling old man whipped a knotted cord around her shoulders and hips, calling out the number of knots it took to circle Alanna to his assistant. Then he laid the cord along the length of her right arm and then her right leg. He sent the anxious-looking apprentice scurrying into a store-room while he measured Coram in the same rapid style. The apprentice returned with an armful of clothing. He was instantly sent after boots and shoes while the grumpy old tailor shook out a gold tunic and held it up to Alanna. The bright garment could have easily fitted a much larger youngster.

Coram fought to hide a grin. "Isn't it a wee bit big?"

The tailor glared at the servingman. "Boys grow," he barked, shoving the whole pile of boots and clothes into Alanna's arms. "It's their natures." He turned his scowl on Alanna. "You rip 'em, you mend 'em," he said. "Don't let me see you for at least three months."

Alanna followed Coram and Timon out, her knees weak with relief. Her secret was still safe!

Timon took them to the huge kitchens for a luncheon and spent the afternoon showing them around the palace. Alanna was lost in no time. She didn't believe Timon when he told her she would soon learn her way around. The royal palace could hold several Trebonds, and more people lived there than Alanna had ever seen before. She learned that many nobles had suites in the palace. There were also quarters for foreign visitors, a servants' wing, the throne and council rooms, ballrooms, kitchens and libraries. It all made her feel extremely small.

The sun was setting as they quickly unpacked. Coram changed into clean clothes in his own room while Alanna slowly laid out her new uniform. She noticed her hands were shaking.

"Alan?" the servingman called.

She opened her door. Coram was ready to go.

"Well, la—lad?" he asked. His dark eyes were kind. "How shall we work this? Th' boys are changin' for dinner."

She tried to smile. "You go on." It was hard making her voice sound relaxed. "I'll be fine."

"You're sure?"

"Of course," she replied stoutly. "Would I have said so if I wasn't?"

"Yes," was the calm answer.

Alanna sighed and rubbed her forehead. She

wished he didn't know her so well. "Best now as later, Coram. I'll be all right. Really. Go on."

He hesitated for a moment. "Good luck—Alan."

"Thanks." She watched him leave and felt lost. Locking the door—it wouldn't do for someone to come in unannounced—she reached for her shirt.

When she was fully dressed, Alanna stared at her reflection in the mirror. She had never looked so fine. The full-sleeved shirt and hose were bright scarlet against the cloth-of-gold tunic. Sturdy leather shoes covered her feet; her dagger and purse hung from a slim leather belt. True, the clothes *were* a little large, but she was too dazzled by the colors to care.

There was one thing to be said for such a bright red and brighter gold: the royal uniform gave her the courage to unbolt the door and step into the hall. She couldn't have done it in her battered old clothes. Several boys saw her and hurried to spread the word: There's a new boy in the palace! Suddenly the pages' wing was very quiet. Everyone came to inspect the newcomer.

Someone behind Alanna grabbed her. She spun. A tall, gangling boy of nearly fourteen looked her over, a sneer on his thick mouth. He had cold blue eyes and sandy-blond hair that flopped over his forehead.

"I wonder what this is." His crooked teeth made him spit his s's. Alanna wiped a drop of saliva from her cheek. "Probably some back-country boy who *thinks* he's a noble."

"Leave him alone, Ralon," someone protested. "He didn't say anything to you."

"He doesn't have to," Ralon snapped. "I bet he's some farmer's son trying to pass for one of us."

Alanna blushed a dull red. "I was told pages were *supposed* to learn manners," she murmured. "Whoever told me that must've been mistaken."

The boy grabbed her collar, lifting her off her feet. "You'll do what you're told," he hissed, "till you earn the right to call yourself a page. If *I* say you're the goatherd's son, *you* say, 'Yes, Lord Ralon.'"

Alanna gasped with fury. "I'd as soon kiss a pig! Is that what *you've* been doing—kissing pigs? Or *being* kissed?"

Ralon threw her against the wall, hard. Alanna charged, ramming into his stomach and knocking him to the floor. Ralon yelled and shoved her off him.

"What is this?"

The young male voice was clear and forceful. Ralon froze; Alanna slowly got to her feet. The watching boys made way for a dark-haired page and his four companions.

Ralon was the first to speak. "Highness, this boy was acting as if he owned the palace," he whined. "King of the castle, he was, and he insulted me like no gentleman insults another—"

"I don't think I spoke to you, Ralon of Malven,"

the boy called "Highness" said. His bright blue eyes fixed on Ralon's. The two boys were about the same height, but the dark-haired boy seemed to be about a year younger and much more commanding. "Unless I'm mistaken, I told you not to talk to me at all."

"But, Highness, he—"

"Shut up, Ralon," instructed one of the boy's friends. This one was big, with tightly curled brown hair and coal-black eyes. "You've got your orders."

Ralon stepped out of the way, red with fury. The boy who seemed to be running things looked around. "Douglass." He nodded to a boy who had been there all along. "What happened?"

A stocky blond page stepped forward. His hair was still wet from washing. He was the one who told Ralon to let Alanna alone.

"It was Ralon, Jon," Douglass said. "The new boy was just standing here. Ralon started on him—called him a country boy, said he was a farmer's son. The new boy said he thought we were here to learn manners. Ralon grabbed him and said the new boy had to do whatever Ralon told him to do, and say 'Yes, Lord Ralon.'"

The boy called Highness looked at Ralon with disgust. "I'm not surprised." He turned his bright eyes back to Alanna. "Then what?"

Douglass grinned. "The new boy said he'd as soon kiss a pig." The pages started to giggle. Alanna blushed and hung her head. Ralon's behavior was bad, but hers wasn't much better. "He said it looked as if Ralon had been kissing pigs. Either that or being kissed himself."

Most of the boys listening laughed outright at this. Alanna could see Ralon's fists clench. She had made her first enemy.

"Ralon threw the boy against the wall," Douglass continued. "The new boy tackled him and knocked him down. That's when you came, Jon."

"I'll speak with you later, Ralon," the dark-haired boy instructed. "In my rooms, before lights-out." When Ralon hesitated, Jon added in a soft, icy voice, "You've been dismissed, Malven."

Ralon hurled himself out of the hallway. The boys watched him go before returning their attention to Alanna. She was still studying the floor.

"You have good taste in enemies, even if you do make them your first day here," Jon said. "Let's have a look at you, Fire-Hair."

Slowly she looked up into his eyes. He was about three years older than she was, with coal-black hair and sapphire-colored eyes. His nose was straight and slightly hooked. His face was stern, but a smile touched his mouth, and a glimmer of fun slipped from his eyes. Alanna linked her hands behind her back, giving him stare for stare until the large boy who had silenced Ralon whispered, "This is Prince Jonathan, lad."

She bowed slightly, afraid that if she bent over any more she would fall. It wasn't every day a person met the heir to the throne. "Your Royal Highness," she said. "I'm sorry about the—the mis-understanding."

"You didn't misunderstand," the Prince told her. "Ralon is no gentleman. What's your name?"

"Alan of Trebond, your Highness."

He frowned. "I don't remember seeing your family at Court."

"No, your Highness."

"Why not?"

"It's my father. He doesn't like it, your Highness."

"I see." There was no way to tell what he thought of her answer. "Do *you* like Court, Alan of Trebond?"

"I don't know," she replied honestly. "I could let you know in a couple of days."

"I look forward to your views." Was he laughing inside? "Have you met the others?"

With royal permission given, the others all tried to introduce themselves at once. The big friendly boy who had given her Jonathan's name was Raoul of Goldenlake. The large young man with chestnut hair and eyes was Gareth—Gary—of Naxen, the Duke's son. The slim, dark boy beside him was Alexander of Tirragen, and Raoul's shy blond shadow was Francis of Nond. There were ten others but these four—and the Prince—were the leaders.

Finally Jonathan said, "Now that we've met our newest member, who will sponsor him?"

Five of the older boys raised their hands. Jonathan nodded. "Your sponsor keeps you from getting too lost," he explained to Alanna. "I think Gary had better take you in hand."

The big youth nodded to Alanna, his brown eyes friendly. "A pleasure."

Alanna bowed politely.

A bell rang. "We'd better go," Jonathan announced. "Alan, stay close to Gary and listen to what he tells you."

Alanna followed her new sponsor to the great dining hall. This was closed only during the summer, when most nobles went to their estates and the rest of the Court went to the Summer Palace by the sea. The other three seasons of the year, the entire Court ate here, served by the pages. Gary stationed Alanna in a niche, where she could see everything. As he hurried back and forth on his serving duties, he whispered explanations to her. It was Gary who showed her to the pages' dining hall after the banquet was over, and Gary who woke her up (she fell asleep over dessert) and guided her to her room.

"Welcome to the palace, young Trebond," he said cheerfully as he handed her over to Coram.

Alanna crawled sleepily into bed, thinking, *Not so bad—for the first day.*

∽

A bell that hung in a tower high over the pages' wing awakened Alanna at dawn. Moaning, she bathed her face in cold water. She was still exhausted from her five-day ride. For once she could have slept late.

Gary—a wide-awake, disgustingly cheerful and large Gary—came for her just as she was finished dressing. When Alanna, who hated breakfast, would have taken only an apple, Gary filled up her plate. "Eat," he advised. "You'll need your strength."

The bell gently chimed. The pages hurried to their first hour of lessons, Alanna trotting to keep up with her sponsor.

"First class is reading and writing," he told her.

"But I know how to read and write!" Alanna protested.

"You do? Good. You'd be surprised at how many noblemen's sons can't. Don't worry, young Trebond." A grin lit his face. "I'm sure the masters will find *some*thing for you to do."

Alanna soon discovered that most of what nobles called "the thinking arts" were taught by Mithran priests. These orange-robed men were stern taskmasters, always quick to catch a boy letting his attention wander or napping. When the priest who taught reading and writing was satisfied that Alanna could do both—he made her read a page from a book aloud, then copy it out on paper—he assigned her a long and very dull poem. Alanna was to read it and be ready to report on it for the next day. The bell rang the hour when she was only partly done.

"When do I finish this?" she asked Gary, waving the scroll on which the poem was written. He was guiding her to their next set of lessons.

"In your free time. Here we go. Mathematics. Can you do figures, too?"

"Some," she admitted.

"A regular scholar," said Alex, who had caught up with them, laughing.

Alanna shook her head. "No. But my father is very strict about book learning."

"He sounds a lot like my father in that respect," Gary said dryly.

"I wouldn't know," Alanna replied. Remembering what the Duke had said about her father the day before, she added, "I don't think they got along."

Again Alanna had to prove her skills, this time to the priest who taught mathematics. Once he was satisfied as to the extent of her knowledge, he put her to learning something called "algebra."

"What is it?" Alanna wanted to know.

The priest frowned at her. "It is a building block," he told her sternly. "Without it you cannot hope to construct a safe bridge, a successful war tower or catapult, a windmill or an irrigation wheel. Its uses are infinite. You will learn them by studying them, not by staring at me."

Alanna *was* staring at him. The idea that mathematics could make things such as windmills and catapults work was amazing. She was even more amazed when she realized how hard the work was that she was supposed to complete for the next day.

When Gary came over to give her a hand, she demanded, "When am I supposed to do this? I have to complete four problems for him by tomorrow, and it's almost time for the next class!"

"In your free time," Gary replied. "And the time you have now. Look—if you get stuck, offer to help Alex with his extra-duty chores. He's a mathematical wizard." The bell rang. "Let's go, youngling."

The next class was in deportment, or manners as they were practiced by nobles. Alanna had learned very early to say "Please" and "Thank you," but she quickly realized that these were only the rudiments of deportment. She did not know how to bow. She did not know how to address a Lord as opposed to an Earl. She did not know which of three spoons to use first at a banquet. She could not dance, and she could not play a musical instrument. The master gave her a very large tome of etiquette to read and ordered her to start lap-harp studies instantly—in her free time.

"But I have to read the first chapter of *this* tonight in my free time!" she told Gary and Alex, thumping the book of etiquette. They were sitting on a bench during their morning break—all ten minutes of it. "And four problems in mathematics, and the rest of that stupid poem—"

"Ah," Gary said dreamily. "'Free time.' I've heard about that. Don't fool yourself, Fire-Top.

What with extra hours of lessons for punishments, *and* the work you get every day, free time is an illusion. It's what you get when you die and the gods reward you for a life spent working from dawn until midnight. We all face up to it sooner or later—the only *real* free time you get here is what my honored sire chooses to give you, when he thinks you have earned it."

"And he doesn't give it to you at night," Alex put in. "He gives it to you when you've been here awhile, on Market Day and sometimes a morning or afternoon all to yourself. But never at night. At night you study. During the day you study. In your sleep—"

The bell rang.

"I could learn to hate that bell," Alanna muttered as she gathered up her things. The older two boys laughed and hurried her along to the next class.

To her surprise, this one was different. The boys sat upright in their chairs, looking as if they were interested in what was about to happen. The walls were hung with maps and charts. A board with several large, blank sheets of paper fixed to it stood before the chairs. A box containing sticks of charcoal for drawing on the paper sat on the table beside it.

The teacher entered to friendly greetings. This man was not a priest. He was short and plump, with long brown hair streaked with gray, and a long shaggy beard. His hose bagged at the knee; his tunic was as rumpled as if he had slept in it. He had a tiny, delicate nose and a smiling mouth. Alanna met the man's large green-brown eyes and smiled in spite of herself. He was the oddest mixture of disarray and good nature she had ever encountered, and she liked him on sight. His name was Sir Myles of Olau.

"Hello," he greeted her cheerfully. "You must be Alan of Trebond. You're very hardy to have made it this far the first day. Has anyone said what we try to learn in here?"

Alanna said the first thing that came to her lips. "The only thing I know is that I jump when I'm told to and I have no free time."

The boys chuckled, and Myles grinned. Alanna blushed. "I'm sorry," she muttered. "I wasn't trying to be pert."

"It's all right," Myles reassured her. "Your life here is going to be difficult. Our Code of Chivalry makes harsh demands."

"Sir Myles, are you going to start on the Code again?" Jonathan asked. "You know we never agree that it asks too much from us."

"No, I'm not going to 'start on' the Code today," Myles replied. "For one thing, you boys won't agree with me until the glamour of being knights and nobles has worn off and you can see the toll our way of life has taken from you. And for another, Duke Gareth has given me to understand that we

are somewhat deficient in our coverage of the
Bazhir Wars and that he hopes to find us more
knowledgeable when next he stops to visit."

"Sir?" someone asked.

Myles looked at Alanna with a twinkle in his
eyes. "I often forget—not everyone is a scholar like
me, and I tend to use obscure language. Therefore,
to translate—Duke Gareth wants me to go over the
Bazhir Wars because he thinks I spent too much
time arguing the Code of Chivalry and not enough
time on the history of Tortall and the history of war-
fare—which *is* what I am supposed to teach you."

Alanna left the class thinking, something she
seldom did seriously.

"Why the frown?" Gary asked, catching up to
her. "Don't you like Myles? I do."

Startled, Alanna blinked at him. "Oh, no. I liked
him a lot. He just seems—"

"Odd," Alex said dryly. He and Gary seemed to
be close friends. "The word you want is 'odd.'"

"Alex and Myles are always arguing about right
and wrong," Gary explained.

"Actually, he seems very wise," Alanna said hesitantly. "Not that I know many wise people, but—"

"He's also the Court drunk," Alex pointed out.
"Come on—before lunch is over and we haven't
eaten."

After lunch came an hour of philosophy.
Alanna almost nodded off to sleep as the teaching
priest droned on about duty.

At last Gary took her outside, down to the acres of practice courts and exercise yards behind the palace. Here was the center of training for knighthood. Alanna would spend her afternoons and part of her evenings here, going inside only when it actually rained or snowed—and sometimes not even then. Here she must learn jousting, fighting with weapons such as maces, axes and staffs, archery while standing and while riding, normal riding and trick riding. She must learn to fall, roll, tumble. She would get dirty, tear muscles, bruise herself, break bones. If she withstood it all, if she was stubborn enough and strong enough, she would someday carry a knight's shield with pride.

Training was endless. Even once a knight had his shield—or her shield—he still worked out in the yards. To get out of shape was to ask for death at the hands of a stranger on a lonely road. As the daughter of a border lord, Alanna knew exactly how important the fighting arts were. Every year Trebond fought off bandits. Occasionally Scanra to the north tried to invade through the Grimhold Mountains, and Trebond was Tortall's first line of defense.

Alanna could already use a bow and a dagger. She was a skilled tracker and a decent rider, but she quickly learned that the men who taught the pages and squires considered her to be a raw beginner.

She *was* a raw beginner. Her afternoon began with an hour of push-ups, sit-ups, jumps and twisting exercises. A knight had to be limber to turn and weave quickly.

For the next hour she wore a suit of padded cloth armor as she received her first lessons with a staff. Before she could learn to use a sword, she had to show some mastery of staff fighting. Without the heavy padding she would have broken something that first afternoon. As it was, she learned to stop a blow aimed at her side, and she felt as if she had been kicked by a horse.

Next she learned the basic movement in hand fighting—the fall. She fell, trying to slap the ground as she hit, trying to take her weight on all the right places and creating new bruises whenever she missed or forgot.

The next hour saw her placing a shield on a bruised and aching left arm. She was paired off with a boy with a stout wooden stick. The purpose of this exercise was to teach her how to use the shield as a defense. If she succeeded, she stopped the oncoming blow. If she didn't, her opponent landed a smarting rap on the part of her she had left exposed. After a while they traded off and she wielded the stick while her partner headed off her attack. This didn't make her feel any better—since she was new to the use of the stick, her opponent caught every strike she tried.

Feeling cheated, Alanna followed Gary to the next yard. Archery was a little better, but only a little. Because she already knew something about archery, she was permitted to actually string the bow and shoot it. When the master discovered she had a good eye and a better aim, he made her work on the way she stood and the way she held her bow—for an hour.

The last hour of her day's studies was spent on horseback. Since Alanna had only Chubby to ride, she was assigned one of the many extra horses kept in the royal stables for some of her riding. Her first lesson was in sitting properly, trotting the horse in a circle, bringing him to a gallop, galloping without falling off and halting the horse precisely in front of the master. Because her horse was too large for her and had a hard mouth, Alanna fell off three times. The beast was impossible for her to control, and when she told the riding master as much, she found herself ordered to report for extra study three nights a week, after the evening meal.

Alanna was staggering with weariness when the distant bell called them inside. She hurried with the others to bathe and change into a clean uniform. By then she was so exhausted she could barely keep her eyes open, but her day wasn't over. Gary shook her out of a snooze and took her down to the banquet hall. He stationed her beside the kitchen door. From this post she handed plates from the kitchen servants to the pages and accepted dirty plates to hand back into the kitchen.

She dozed off during her meal. Gary steered her to a small library afterward, reminding her of the studying she had to do for the next day. He helped her with the poem, then left her on her own to deal with the mathematics. Alanna fought her way through three of the problems before going to sleep on the desk. A servant found her and roused her just in time for lights-out. She fell into bed and was instantly asleep.

Waking the next morning, Alanna moaned. Every muscle in her body was stiff and sore. She was speckled with large and small bruises. Stiffly she got ready for the new day, wondering if she would live through it.

It was like the day before, only worse. The mathematics master assigned her an additional four problems for that day, plus three more—punishment for the problem she had left undone during her nap the night before. The reading master informed her that since her oral report on the long poem was inadequate, she could put a longer report in writing—for the next day. The master in deportment gave her yet another chapter to read in etiquette and made her practice bows the whole period. The afternoon was hideous. Because she was stiff and aching, Alanna made more mistakes than she had the day before. She found herself with more extra work.

"Face it," Gary told her kindly. "You'll never catch up. You just do as much as you can and take the punishments without saying anything. Sometimes I wonder if that isn't what they're really trying to teach us—to take plenty and keep our mouths shut."

Alanna was in no mood to consider this idea. When she returned to her rooms that night, she was tired, nervous and upset.

"Pack your things," she ordered Coram as she marched in the door. "We're going home."

Coram looked at her. He had been sitting on his bed, cleaning his sword. "We are?"

Alanna paced the room. "I can't do this," she told the manservant. "The pace will kill me. No one can live this way all the time. I won't—"

"I never figured ye for a quitter," Coram interrupted softly.

"I'm not quitting!" Alanna snapped. "I—I'm protesting! I'm protesting unfair treatment—and—and being worked till I drop. I want to have time to myself. I want to learn to fight with a sword *now*, not when they decide. I want—"

"Ye want. Ye want. 'Tis something different ye're learning here. It's called 'discipline.' The world won't always order itself the way *ye* want. Ye have to learn discipline."

"This isn't discipline! It's inhuman! I can't live with it, and I won't! Coram, I gave you an order! Pack your things!"

Coram carefully scrubbed a tiny bit of dirt off his gleaming sword. At last he put it down, carefully, on the bed. With a groan he knelt down and reached under the bed, dragging out his bags. "As ye say," he replied. "But I thought I'd raised ye with somethin' to ye. I didn't think I was bringin' up another soft noble lady—"

"I'm not a soft noble lady!" Alanna cried. "But I'm not crazy, either! I'm going from sunrise to sunset and after without a stop, and no end in sight. My free time's a joke—I'm out of free time before I get to the third class of the morning. And they expect me to keep up, and they punish me if I don't. And I have to learn how to fall; I'm learning the stance with the bow all over again when I was the best hunter at Trebond, and if I say *anything* I get more work!"

Coram knelt on the floor, looking at her. "Ye knew it'd be hard when ye decided to come," he reminded her. "No one ever told ye a knight had it easy. *I* didn't, for certain. I told ye 'twas naught but hard work every wakin' minute, and a lot of extra wakin' minutes to boot. And now ye're runnin' away after just two days of it."

"I'm not running away!"

"As ye say, Mistress." Coram hoisted himself onto the bed with a groan, reaching for his boots. "I'll be packed as soon as may be."

Alanna slammed into her own room. She yanked one of her bags out and stared at it. With a sigh she sat down, rubbing her head in disgust. At Trebond she could come and go as she pleased, do as she liked. Life here was completely different. Did that make it bad?

She wasn't sure any longer. Coram's words about "quitting" and "running away" stuck like barbs under her skin. She tried to tell herself she *wasn't* running away, but she wasn't having much success.

At last she opened her door and looked out at Coram. "All right," she growled. "I'll give it a week. No more and no less. It had better lighten up by then."

"Ye're the Mistress—or the Master," Coram replied. "But if ye're goin' to go—"

"I'll make the decisions," she told him. "Now, good night!"

It wasn't until she pulled the blankets over her that she realized Coram had put his bags back under the bed and removed his boots. The old soldier had not done any packing at all.

I wish he didn't know me so well, she thought grumpily as she dozed off.

The one week became two weeks, the two weeks became three, and Alanna was too exhausted to think of the long ride home. She never caught up with her work, and every day at least one master found something not done and gave her still more to do. She learned to take Gary's advice, doing as much as she could each day and taking her punishments without complaint.

Her first night of table service came and went. She was too tired to be afraid during this first test. She waited on Duke Gareth, listened to his lecture on table manners and continued to serve at the banquets. At last she was assigned permanently to wait on Sir Myles, much to her delight. The knight always had something kind to say, even if—as Alex had said—he *did* drink too much. Sometimes she even helped him back to his rooms if he had drunk too well. Often he would give her a silver penny, or a sweet, and his classes were the bright point in her morning. Myles had a knack for making history seem real.

She and Gary quickly became friends. Gary always had something funny to say about the master of deportment, and he was never too busy to give her a hand, if she could bring herself to ask for help. She also discovered she could make her large friend laugh simply by saying whatever came to her mind. She liked making someone as intelligent as Gary laugh.

Between Gary, Myles and other people in the palace, life got better. Alanna came to forget that she had once ordered Coram to pack and take her home.

ᖇᖇ

*T*hree months—and her eleventh birthday— passed before Alanna realized it. The first break in her new routine came one night when Timon came hunting for her.

"He wants to see you." Timon never had to say who "he" was. "You're to go to his study."

Alanna straightened her tunic and tried to

smooth her hair before rapping on Duke Gareth's door. Why would the Duke want to see her? What had she done wrong?

He called for her to come in, looking up from his papers as she closed the door behind her. "Alan, come in. I'm writing your father, reporting on your progress. Do you have any messages for me to send to him?"

She wasn't in trouble! Alanna smothered a sigh of relief. Then she thought of something worse. What if her father came out of his studious fog and actually *read* Duke Gareth's letter?

I'll think of that when it happens, she told herself. Would things ever get easy?

"Please say that I send my regards, sir," she told the Duke.

The man put down his quill pen. "My report is satisfactory. You learn well and quickly. We are glad to have you among us."

Alanna turned pink with delight. She had never received such a high compliment. "Th-thank you, your Grace!"

"You may go to the City tomorrow morning as a reward. In future, you may also go there with the other pages on Market Day. Since you're new to Corus, you may have one of the older boys accompany you. Not Alex. He has to take an extra hour of Ethics tomorrow."

Alanna beamed. "You're very kind," she said. "Uh—could Gary—Gareth—come?"

The Duke raised an eyebrow. "Hm. He *did* say you are good company. It can be arranged. Be certain to return in time for afternoon lessons."

"Yes, sir!" She bowed deeply, "And thank you again!"

∽

Gary had to laugh at Alanna's wide eyes as they walked through the city's marketplace. "Close your mouth, country boy," he teased. "Most of this is overpriced."

"But there's so much of everything!" she exclaimed.

"Not here. One of these days we'll ride to Port Caynn. You'll see *real* wonders there." He stopped to look at a pair of riding gloves. Alanna wistfully eyed the long sword that hung beside them. She would need a sword someday. How would she ever get a good one?

A large hand tapped her shoulder. Startled, she looked up into the hazel eyes of the man Coram had called a thief just three months before.

"So—it's the young sprout with the purple eyes," the man said pleasantly. "I was wonderin' if you'd fallen into a well." His voice was rough and uneducated, but he spoke carefully. To Alanna it seemed that he thought about every word before saying it.

She grinned at him. Somehow this meeting didn't surprise her. "I've been at the palace."

"Who's your friend?" Gary asked, looking at Alanna's acquaintance suspiciously.

"Allow me to introduce myself, young masters." The man bowed. "I'm George Cooper, of the lower city. Will you take a cool drink with me? As my guests, of course."

"Thank you," Alanna said quickly. "We accept."

George took them to a little inn called the Dancing Dove. The old man who ran it greeted him like a good friend, hurrying to bring ale for George and lemonade for the pages. When the drinks came, Alanna examined George as she gulped her lemonade. George said he was seventeen, although he seemed older. His nose was too big for good looks, but when he smiled he appeared handsome. He wore his brown hair cut short, like other commoners. Alanna felt something powerful about him, something almost royal. She also felt a very strong liking for him.

"You shouldn't be surprised at my lookin' you up," he told Alanna. "Truth to tell, I like your looks. We don't see many with eyes like yours. You bein' from the country—you don't look it now, but you did then!—I thought you'd like to be knowin' someone in the city."

"Do you always make friends on such short notice?" Gary asked sharply.

George looked at him a moment. "I trust my instincts, young master. In my line of work, you learn quick to trust your instincts."

"What is it you do, George?" Alanna wanted to know.

George winked at her. "I—buy, and I sell."

"You're a thief," Gary said flatly.

"'Thief' is a harsh word, Master Gareth." He looked at the big youth. "Why would you be thinkin' that I am? You've still got your purse, and what's in it. Or you had better."

Gary checked and admitted, "I still have my purse. But why do you want to make friends with us? If you think we'll help you in the palace, you're wrong. Don't you know who I am?"

George met Gary's eyes, and in them saw clearly a great intelligence. One could sense that the boy had made enemies with his sharp mind and sharper tongue.

George read some of this, then relaxed. "I know well you're Gareth of Naxen, the Duke's son. I didn't look you up for professional reasons. Truth to tell, were you not with Alan, I wouldn't have put myself in your way. We're not fond of nobles here." His smile twisted. "But I've the Gift. It helps me see more clearly than most. I knew I must meet Master Alan. In fact, I've kept a close eye on him these three months. I don't ignore my Gift when it calls me."

Gary shrugged. "I don't know much about magic, but that makes sense. Still—what can *Alan* do for you? He's just a little guy." Gary grinned an apology to Alanna, who shrugged. She was getting used to such remarks. "And unless I miss my guess, you're the man the Lord Provost would most love to get his hands on."

George nodded respectfully. "You're quick, Master Gary. All right, then. I'm what they call the King of the Thieves, the Master of the Court of the Rogue. The Court of the Rogue," he explained to Alanna, "is all of us who make our livin' by our wits. It's ruled by a king—me, right now. Sometimes he's called just 'the Rogue.' But mastery don't last very long here. Who knows when some young buck will do for me what *I* did for the King before me, just six months back? I'll need friends, when that comes." He shrugged. "Still, it won't happen soon. Till then, why look a gift thief in the mouth? I can be a good friend to those who keep faith with me."

Gary looked him over, then nodded. "I like you—for all you're a thief."

George laughed. "And I like you, Gary—for all you're a noble. Friends, then?"

"Friends," Gary said firmly. They shook hands across the table.

"And you, Alan?" George asked. Alanna had been watching and thinking, none of her thoughts clear on her small face. With his magic, would George know her secret? Then she remembered what Maude had taught her—having the Gift instantly shielded you from the magic vision of someone else with the Gift. For the moment

George wouldn't be able to guess her secret, and even if he did, Alanna suspected a thief wouldn't tell his own mother the time of day unless he had a good reason.

"I'd like some more lemonade," she said, pouring her tankard full. "The Gift must be pretty useful to you."

"It's gotten me out of more than one tight place," George admitted. "It helps me keep tabs on my rogues, so maybe I'll last longer than the king before me." He drained his own tankard and set it down. "You need never worry about your pockets, or those of the friends you bring here. But be careful who you bring. One word from them and my Lord Provost gets my head for certain."

"We'll be careful," Gary promised. "Don't worry about Alan. He keeps his mouth shut."

George grinned. "As I can see. Few sprouts— even ones sealed to the Rogue—could listen to all this and say nothing. Well, you'd best be gettin' back. If you need anything, send word through Stefan—he works in the palace stables. You'll find me here most of the time, and if not, ask old Solom." He jerked a thumb at the innkeeper. "He'll fetch me quick enough."

Alanna rose. She and Gary shook hands with their new friend. "You'll be seeing us, then," she promised. "Good day to you."

The two pages strolled out into the street. The King of the Thieves watched them go, smiling.

⚭

Several weeks later Duke Gareth called Alanna out of her mathematics class. Confused, she went to meet him.

He handed her a letter. "Can you explain this?"

Alanna scanned the much-blotted parchment. It was from her father. The letter was short, saying only that he trusted Thom would continue to do well.

Luckily she had her story planned. Looking up, she shrugged, her face a little sad. "He forgets, you see, I don't think he's ever been able to tell my brother and I—"

"My brother and *me*," the Duke corrected sternly.

"My brother and me," she repeated obediently, "apart." She crossed her fingers behind her back and tried a guess. "I don't think he even let His Majesty know when we were born."

The Duke thought this over and nodded. "You're right—he didn't. He hasn't changed." The man sighed. "I hope your brother does as well as you. If your father cannot tell you apart, at least he can be proud of both of his sons."

Alanna hung her head, hating herself for having to lie to someone like Duke Gareth. "Thank you, your Grace," she whispered.

"You may go. Don't forget to write your father yourself."

Alanna bowed. "Of course, sir." She let herself out and closed the door. In the corridor she sagged against the wall. With luck, now Duke Gareth would believe all such letters were due to Lord Alan's bad memory.

She returned to her class, still feeling wobbly. There were real advantages to having a father who didn't care what she did.

But if the advantages were so wonderful, why did she feel like crying?

three

Ralon

Alanna had not forgotten Ralon of Malven, and he had not forgotten her. Usually they didn't meet, since he was beginning his training as a squire while Alanna was training as a page. When they did meet, Ralon made it clear they were enemies. He was simply awaiting his chance to get her.

On summer afternoons squires and pages alike ended their lessons with swimming as well as riding. They returned to the palace one such afternoon later than usual. Most of the boys hurried to their rooms to wash up. Alanna was wiping down her pony when she heard a thud. Ralon stood outside Chubby's stall. His saddle and bridle lay on the ground.

"Curry my horse and hang these up," he ordered. "I'm going in."

Alanna stared at him. "You're joking."

Ralon shoved her into Chubby. "I said *do* it."

Before she could recover her breath, he was gone. She stared after him, clenching and unclenching her fists. She wanted to kill him!

"Are ye goin' t' do it?"

Alanna looked up, startled. George's man, the hostler Stefan, swung down from the hayloft above. He was a short, blond youth with pale eyes and reddish skin. Animals loved him, and he was more comfortable with horses than with people, but he seemed to like Alanna and her friends well enough.

It took her a moment to make her voice work. "What?"

"Are ye goin' t' clean up after yon?" Stefan spat, hitting Chubby's manger squarely.

Alanna looked at the saddle and drew a breath. Now that she had to take a stand, she was just as scared as she was angry. "No. I can't. I won't."

Stefan shrugged. "I'll have t' tell his Grace, y'know," he reminded her. "It's orders. Th' lads must look after they own beasts. His Grace must know if they don't."

Alanna hesitated. Ralon would murder her. But—if she knuckled under, Ralon would do this all the time.

"Tell," she said gruffly, going back to work on Chubby. "It's not my problem."

"Think on it," Stefan advised, worry on his round face. "That Ralon won't like bein' in trouble wiv his Grace."

Alanna looked up from her pony, her eyes flat violet. "That's Ralon's lookout, isn't it?" she asked softly. She finished combing Chubby and left.

Stefan shook his head. *Th' lad's got guts*, he thought. *Not much sense, but guts.*

By bedtime that night the word was out: Ralon had to spend his nights for a month working in the stables. Jonathan's friends had trouble hiding their glee.

"Serves him right," Francis remarked. They were sitting in Gary's room before lights-out. "He just left his tack on the ground. His horse was covered with sweat. That's no way to treat a good horse."

"I wonder how he thought he could get away with it?" Alex murmured.

"He probably tried to make some little guy do it," Raoul said with contempt. "Isn't that his usual?"

Alanna had been permitted to join them. Now she turned red and looked down at the lacings on her shoes.

Gary saw the blush. "Alan—you were the last one in this afternoon. Do you know about this?"

Alanna didn't approve of lying, but in a pinch a lie was sometimes better than the truth. "No."

Raoul grinned. "I'd like to see him mess with our Alan. I'd pound him to a pulp." Alanna had become a favorite with Raoul, and he didn't care who knew it.

Alanna made a face. "I do my own fighting, thanks."

"Raoul just wants an excuse," Jonathan explained. "He *likes* hitting Ralon."

"Ralon didn't make anyone else put his tack

away?" Alex wanted to know. "You didn't see anything strange?"

Alanna didn't look up. "No." *It wasn't strange*, she excused her lie mentally. *Ralon does things like that all the time.*

The servants arrived, sending the boys off to bed. Jonathan returned to his room, frowning thoughtfully. Trouble was brewing between Ralon and the boy Alan, but there didn't seem to be anything he could do to stop it.

His punishment didn't keep him from the afternoon rides, so Ralon was with the boys at the swimming hole the next day. The weather was hot and damp. Most of the boys stripped down to their loincloths and leaped into the pool. Alanna sat under a shady tree, looking wistfully at her friends. She would have loved to join them.

Ralon planted himself in front of her. "Too good for us, Master Alan? Afraid to get in the same water with us?"

Alanna looked up. The others were suddenly quiet.

"Leave me alone," she snapped.

"'Leave me alone,'" he mocked, swinging his hips. "Too good to swim with us, Alan the Snot?"

"I don't feel like swimming." The others were watching her, wondering if she was a coward. *He'll kill me*, she thought. *I'm just a girl, and he'll kill me.*

Ralon grabbed her arm. "Into the water, page," he gritted. "We'll have some fun."

Alanna rammed herself into Ralon's stomach. The older boy yelped as he tumbled into the pool, hitting the water with a painful smack.

"Why, Ralon," cried Raoul. "Let me help you up!" Seizing one of Ralon's flailing arms, the bigger youth yanked Ralon's legs from under him. Ralon sank to the bottom with Raoul on top of him. He struggled frantically, but Raoul was impossible to budge. When Ralon finally surfaced, he was half blind and three-quarters drowned. He glared at the wickedly grinning Raoul.

"Malven!" Alanna shouted. She was standing, her fists tight against her sides. "I don't like to swim. Don't try to get me in the water again! And don't order me around, either! The next time you try it, I'll break your face! D'you hear me?"

Jonathan put a hand on Ralon's shoulder. "You heard Alan," the Prince whispered. "Don't forget." He shoved Ralon under the water again.

Alanna returned to her seat. Ralon wouldn't forget this, but there was no sense in worrying about trouble until it happened.

That evening she was serving Sir Myles when Ralon passed her. Under the noise of serving he whispered, "Part payment, snot," and pinched her viciously.

Alanna dropped the plate she was holding, biting back a yell of pain. She cleaned up the mess, blinking away tears of rage, knowing she would catch it later from Duke Gareth.

"Everyone slips," Myles told her kindly.

"Uh—Alan—I feel a little tired. Would you be so good as to escort me to my chambers after the King rises?"

She nodded, puzzled. Myles had been drinking lightly this evening. Unless he was drunk, he never asked her to walk him to his rooms.

As she suspected, Myles didn't need assistance. Once at his rooms, however, he stopped her as she turned to go. "A moment, Alan, if you please."

Alanna took the seat he pointed to, wondering what he wanted.

The knight lit a branch of candles and put it on the table between her chair and his. He poured himself a glass of brandy, nodding to a bowl of fruit. "Help yourself. I'll try not to keep you from your dinner too long."

"Thank you, sir." Alanna took an orange and began peeling it.

"Young Ralon is picking on you, isn't he?"

Alanna froze. "I don't know what you mean, sir."

"Don't be coy, Alan."

"Sir?"

"Don't hide something we're both aware of. I see much of what goes on here. It's one reason I drink so much. And I see Ralon bullying you when you're alone or with the younger boys."

Alanna shrugged. "I'm not a crybaby or a telltale."

"Do you think you'll lose the other boys' respect if you say anything? Prince Jonathan would be the first to take your side."

Alanna felt very uncomfortable. "I have to handle this myself."

Myles shook his head. "What are you trying to prove?" he asked. She refused to answer. He went on bitterly, "I truly love our Code of Chivalry. We are taught that noblemen must take everything and say nothing. Noblemen must stand alone. Well, we're men, and men aren't born to stand alone."

"Nobles are," Alanna replied. "Or they have to. Isn't that the same thing?"

Myles shook his head. "No, it isn't." He sighed. "You'll have to fight him in the end."

"I know, sir."

"Alan, he's taller and heavier than you! He'll kill you!"

Alanna put her orange aside. "Then I fight him till he lets me alone or till I get big enough to beat him. I can't let him walk all over me, Sir Myles! When you're—" She stopped, horrified. She had almost admitted she was a girl! She rushed on. "When you're little, like me, you either quit and get picked on all the time, or you stick it out. I have to stick it out."

Myles made a face. "Run along to your supper." She got up to go. "Alan."

"Sir?"

"If you have to hit—hit low."

She grinned and bowed. "Thanks, Sir Myles. I'll keep that in mind."

∾

*T*rouble came the next day, in the stables. Alanna was there grooming Chubby; the others were gone. She was dreaming of the horse she would someday own when she heard the stable door creak.

An ugly sneer twisted Ralon's face. "I suppose you think our talk yesterday was the last one."

Alanna was shaking with nervous energy. "No," she said flatly.

Ralon swaggered around her, eyeing her stocky form. "You're too big for your breeches. You aren't so much when you don't have Raoul or Gary to hide behind, are you?"

She clenched her fists. "I don't hide behind anyone," she retorted. "And I don't have to pick on someone littler'n me to prove what a man I am, either!"

He grabbed her shoulders, shaking her hard. "I won't take that from you, dunghill trash!"

She hit low and hard. Ralon doubled over, clutching his lower belly. She waited, legs braced, fists ready. "Take it back. Or I'll stuff your mouth with dung—since you like it so much!"

∾

*M*ercifully no one saw her when she returned. Alanna closed her door and bolted it, keeping her head down. Coram had her bath waiting.

"Mother of Darkness," he whispered when he saw her. "What happened?"

She glanced at the mirror. Her uniform was a bloody, dirty mess. "I fell down."

Coram forced her to look up at him. She flinched as he wiped her face with a wet cloth. His callused hands were surprisingly gentle. "It's lyin' ye are. Ye were in a fight."

"I said I fell down." She gasped as he touched her eye.

"Ah. The ground bloodied yer nose, split yer lip and punched ye in th' eye, all to once. Would ye prefer to say 'twas yer pony? Th' others didn't say ye were hurt, so ye must've—fallen—in th' stables."

"I don't want to talk about it," she said coldly.

He grinned. "I'm off t' fetch some raw meat for yer eye where th' ground hit ye. I'll tell th' lads ye're ill." He clapped her on the shoulder and added gruffly, "Ye're a plucky lass. I'm proud of ye. And I think it's time I gave ye a bit of help."

She lay down after he left. Tears forced themselves from her eyes. This wouldn't have happened to a *real* boy.

Someone tapped on the door. "Alan? It's Raoul. Coram says you're sick. What's wrong?"

"Nothing."

"Can we come in?"

"No! Go away!"

"Alan—it's Alex. What's the matter?"

"There's nothing the matter!" she yelled. "Just leave me alone!"

Brief silence.

"Alan. Open the door." This was the Prince, and he was giving an order.

Slowly she obeyed. It was nearly dark—maybe they wouldn't notice.

All her friends were standing outside. She looked at the floor. "I—I'm sorry I yelled. It's just the heat, I guess—"

"Look at me," Jonathan commanded.

That she would not do. He put cool fingers beneath her chin and lifted her face. She gave him look for look with her good eye, ignoring the gasps and murmurs of pity.

"What happened?" the Prince asked finally.

"I fell down, Highness. In the stables." Now they all knew what a weakling she was.

Jonathan let her go. "I'll make your excuses to Uncle Gareth. We'll bring you something to eat later."

"Thank you," she whispered. "I'm not hungry."

"Here, lads—what's this?" Coram was returning with a slice of raw meat. "Alan had a bit of an accident, that's all. Ye'd best be gettin' to th' tables— his Majesty's about to start."

The others hurried away. Jonathan hesitated. "I'll be back," he told Coram.

The man bowed. "Very good, yer Highness."

❧

That night the pages ate in silence. After dinner Jonathan and his friends went to Gary's rooms.

"It was Ralon!" Raoul burst out when they were alone.

"He didn't like what happened yesterday," Francis pointed out.

"It's time we dealt with him," Alex added in his soft voice. "He forgets his place."

"I'll teach it to him," Raoul growled.

"He forgot the lesson you taught him yesterday," Gary reminded him.

Raoul smiled coldly. "This time I'll make sure he knows what the lesson's about."

"You're forgetting something." They all looked at Jonathan. "Alan won't admit Ralon hit him. He wants to fight Ralon himself."

"He can't," Raoul protested. "He's just a little guy. And he doesn't know how to fight!"

"He's got courage," Alex said.

"Courage!" Raoul bellowed. "That coward almost *kills* him and—"

"Hush!" Jonathan ordered. "Listen. We must be sure. Gary—see if anyone at the stables knows what happened. Perhaps Alan will tell me something. And remember—we have to do it his way. He'd be ashamed if he thought we were fighting his battles."

The others nodded agreement, and the group split up.

⌒

"*H*ow do you feel?" the Prince asked.

Alanna struggled to sit up. "Miserable, Highness," she admitted.

"Poor little man. He really whipped you, didn't he?"

"Nobody whipped me. I fell."

He grinned. "Deny it all you want. We both know you had a fight with Ralon and you lost."

She stuck her chin out stubbornly. "I fell. Your Highness."

Jonathan patted her shoulder. "You're pluck to the backbone, young Trebond. Get some sleep."

∽

Gary found Stefan immediately. The hostler nodded as the young nobleman climbed into his hayloft. "I thought perhaps one o' ye would be comin' around. What lie is Master Alan tellin'?"

Gary made a face. "He says he fell down."

Stefan spat. "Oh, aye, he fell. O' course, Master Ralon helped him fall, several times. Poor li'l tyke didn't have a chance." He chuckled. "But he got Master Malven a good 'un in th' nuts t' start."

"Why didn't you stop them?" Gary wanted to know.

Stefan shook his head. "It's th' rules—we don't mess in th' nobles' fights. But I'll say this—if Ralon ever comes back from th' City wiv a full purse, George'll have all our ears. George likes Master Alan."

"Let George do what he wants." Then Gary frowned. "What do you mean, he'll have your ears?"

Stefan's eyes were calm. "George has a collection. One slip an' he warns ye. Two, an' he takes an ear—fer his collection. Three mistakes—" Stefan shrugged. "He takes t'other ear an' all that's attached. George likes things done right."

ᔑᨄ

The next afternoon Raoul beat Ralon thoroughly. Ralon broke the code and informed Duke Gareth. From then on Jonathan's friends left any room Ralon entered. Raoul watched Ralon all the time, just waiting for his chance.

Ralon couldn't take revenge on Raoul, or Gary, or the Prince. Instead he found an easier victim.

"You told your friends!" he hissed when he caught Alanna in the library alone one day. He blacked her other eye and split her lip again. Four days later he caught her once more. This time Alanna used a few tricks Coram had taught her. She bloodied Ralon's nose.

Ralon broke her arm.

Each talk she had with Duke Gareth was worse than the last one. Once again she faced him, this time with one arm in a sling.

"I fell down, your Grace," she said, her face straight.

"Mithros, boy—can't you think of a better excuse?"

She scuffed a foot. "This one works so well, sir. It—it has tradition behind it."

Gareth scowled at her. "It certainly does. I've heard it from every page who's been fighting that I ever trained—with a few exceptions."

"Well, sir, you don't believe me and I *know* you don't believe me, but pride is satisfied all around. Your Grace."

The Duke had to hide a smile. "You are pert, Alan of Trebond. An extra hour of mathematics for you for the next five weeks. You may go."

Alanna was opening the door when he added, "I wish you would thrash him. He deserves it."

She looked back at him. "I will one day, sir. I'm getting tired of falling down."

While Alanna talked to Duke Gareth, Stefan came to the practice courts in search of the master who was teaching the boys hand-to-hand combat. After Stefan lured the teacher away, Jonathan's friends surrounded Ralon. He saw Raoul adjusting the padded gloves on his big hands and began to sweat.

Jonathan spoke, his voice icy. "You were warned, Malven. You are no gentleman. You are a dog, and you shall be thrashed like one."

Gary held Ralon. Raoul administered the beating, his face impossible to read. When the boys' teacher returned from his wild-goose chase, he found his students practicing wrestling. Ralon, they said, was sick and had gone to his room.

After that Ralon kept to small bits of nastiness, knowing Alanna would never complain to anyone. If she had gone swimming, the others would have seen the many bruises on her body. As it was, she said nothing and continued to study with Coram. She lived with Ralon's tormenting and spent her free time wrestling and boxing. She fell asleep the moment she rolled into bed, only to rise at dawn to practice some more. She was determined to beat Ralon—it would mean she had finally earned her place among the boys. It would mean that she could do anything larger and stronger males could.

Her splinted arm turned into an advantage. Normally she was right-handed. Now Alanna had to depend on her left hand for everything, and her left hand was the one she first learned to really fight with. She quickly saw that she could be twice as effective using both hands, and worked as hard as she could to develop her skill.

In mid-October the palace healers removed the splint. If they were surprised that her arm had healed so quickly, they said nothing. Impatient to get Ralon, Alanna had used her Gift to help mend her broken bone.

In bed the night the splint was taken off, she waited to hear Coram's snores before getting up. Quickly she put on dark clothes and picked up her boots. She crept through Coram's room, trying not to make a sound.

When she got to the door, Coram sighed, "*Now* what are ye up to?"

Alanna froze. "Go back to sleep."

"Where are ye goin'?" She could see him sitting up in the dim light from the window.

"If Duke Gareth asks, you won't be lying when you say you don't know," she pointed out.

Coram made a resigned noise. "Lass—it's restriction to the palace if ye're caught."

"I know."

"All right, then. I won't bolt the door." He lay back down and immediately went back to sleep.

It was easy to slip out of the palace and onto the road to the city. Alanna set off at a jog-trot, wishing she was riding Chubby. Still, she knew she couldn't have ridden out of the palace without being spotted.

The Dancing Dove was bustling. She could barely see through the smoke-filled air, and the noise of the thieves and their ladies having fun was deafening. For a moment she wanted to turn and run, but Ralon was waiting back at home. Better to face George's friends—who were *honest* villains— than Ralon the sneak. But how was she to find George in this mess?

A tall, chesty redhead stopped and looked Alanna over. Planting her hands firmly on her hips, the redhead drawled, "A bit young for this place, aren't you, sonny?"

Her husky voice was teasing, but there was kindness in the lady's large brown eyes. "I'm looking for George," Alanna replied. "He said I could find him here."

The woman made a face. "He did? That sounds like him, tellin' a bit of a boy t' come t' this place at night."

"I don't think he expected me to come at

night," Alanna said, always fair.

"Humph. Wait," the woman ordered. She vanished into the crowded room, to return within minutes. "Come on, then—and have an eye t' your purse."

"I didn't bring one," Alanna yelled above the din as she followed the redhead.

"Here you be." The woman shoved Alanna into a clear space before the fire. A table had been set beside the hearth and George sat at its head. Gathered around him were men and women who eyed Alanna curiously.

George had an odd expression in his eyes as he looked her over. Finally he spoke. "Alan, this is Rispah, the Queen of the ladies who follow the Rogue. Alan's a friend of mine—from the country."

Rispah gave a crooked grin. "I'm sure he is." Raising her voice, she called, "Solom, you old dotard, bring lemonade for the boy. Can't you see he's parched?" She looked at Alanna. "Unless you want somethin' stronger, youngling?"

Alanna turned bright red. "No, thank you."

Rispah went back to her friends. Alanna remained standing. Why was George looking at her so strangely?

At last the man said, "I hear you're havin' trouble with the Malven."

"That's one way of putting it," she agreed. *I shouldn't have come,* she thought.

Solom appeared with a tankard of lemonade.

"Welcome back, Master Alan." He smiled. "I see yer arm be healed."

"Good as new. Thanks, Solom." She accepted the tankard and looked at George. "May I?"

"Yes, of course. Sit down."

Alanna clenched one hand behind her back. Here came the hard part. "Actually—can we go talk alone?" She drew a deep breath. Asking for things was not easy. "I—I need a favor."

George stood, grim faced. "We'll go to my chambers." He put an arm around her shoulders and added, "Solom, we're not to be disturbed."

The innkeeper nodded. "As ye say, Majesty."

George climbed a narrow staircase leading upstairs, Alanna following. "They call you 'Majesty'?" she asked, shocked.

"Why not? I'm king here—more king than the man who sits atop the big hill. My people wouldn't give *him* a word in passing, but they follow my slightest wish."

"I suppose," she said doubtfully.

George unlocked a sturdy door. "You're careless, young Alan, but you're polite." He inspected each corner of his two rooms before waving her inside. "Sit." He lit a branch of candles from the torch in the hall before closing the door. Alanna looked around at the plain wood furniture, noting how neat and clean the room was. She also noted that the candlestick George placed on the table was silver, while the frame on the mirror hanging on his bedroom door was wrought gold.

The thief settled his length into one of the chairs by the table while Alanna took another. "Why am I careless?" she wanted to know. "I made sure no one saw me leave the palace."

The funny look was still in George's eyes. "Humph." He did not sound convinced. "A favor, you say. What's it to be? A throat cutting? Some of my bully boys taking Ralon into an alley for a chat?"

Alanna stood, shoving her chair from the table so hard that it fell over. "If *that's* what you think I want, I'm off," she snapped. "I—I thought—" She bit a trembling lip. How could he *think* she would make such a disgraceful request?

"Easy, lad. Here." George picked up the chair and pressed her back into it. "I misjudged you. Forgive me. I've known many nobles who take advantage. How was I to know you aren't one of them?"

Alanna frowned, puzzled. "What d'you mean, 'nobles who take advantage'?"

George sighed and sat down. "I've known nobles who thought I should be grateful for their friendship—grateful enough to do them all sorts of favors. They wanted a kept thief, not a friend. I thought at first that's what you came for. Now I see you're here as a friend, askin' a friend's help. It isn't a beatin' for Ralon that you want? It's a beatin' he needs."

"That's what I want," she said grimly, "but *I* want to be the one to beat him."

"Better and better. Why come to me, then?"

She stared at her hands. "Coram's been teaching me boxing and wrestling, but Ralon already knows those things. He's a squire. I hoped you might know some hand fighting they don't teach us at the palace."

George thought about this. "Haven't they a Shang master up there? The Shangs know more tricks than anyone can hope to learn—unless you started as young as they do."

Alanna shook her head. "The last Shang master left a few days after I arrived. Sir Myles says they don't like to settle down."

George nodded. "He's right. They wander from the day they leave Shang till the day they die. Peculiar folk, Shang warriors. So." He leaned back, watching her. "Why d'you think I can teach you better than a man who cut his eyeteeth on a sword?"

"But that's it. Coram is a swordsman. I bet you win *your* fights bare-handed, or with a knife."

George grinned. "You're right at that." He stood, removing his vest and boots. "Take off your cloak, then, and the shoes. Your first lesson starts now."

∾

*F*or weeks Alanna worked with Coram and George. She began to surprise her masters with her ability to keep going when bigger boys were exhausted. Alanna's silence bothered Ralon, but he never realized what she planned for him. He continued to pester her when he got the chance; and when a chance didn't turn up, he made his opportunities. Alanna said nothing. She knew the older boys suspected the feud was still going on, but this was *her* fight. She would show everyone—including that part of her that was always wondering—that she was as good as any boy in the palace.

Shortly before Midwinter Festival, in December, Alanna was relaxing with George after a lesson. The thief pushed a tankard of ale at her. "Drink up," he ordered. "Are you waitin' till you're a man grown before you give Malven what's comin' to him?"

Until now George had never let her have anything but lemonade. "You think I'm ready?" she asked in a very small voice.

"'Tis not my opinion that matters. The only way you'll win is if *you* think you're ready."

She saw what he meant. Smiling grimly, she raised her tankard to him and drank the ale down.

The next day all the boys were exercising in the indoor practice courts. Alanna watched Ralon all afternoon as she waited for her chance. She was scared: her face felt hot, her hands shook. If she failed, she would leave Court. She couldn't be a knight if Ralon continued to beat on her. And today was her day. She had never felt so strong and so prepared.

The teachers left. Ralon was in a corner, punching a straw dummy. Alanna drew a deep breath and walked out into the center of the floor.

She announced clearly, "Ralon of Malven has beggars and thieves for ancestors." *Excuse me, George,* she added silently. "He's the son of a lizard and a demon. He has all the honor of a weasel. He can't even fight in the open like a man and a noble. He picks his fights in back halls—so no one can see him cheat."

The boys were open-mouthed with surprise. Suddenly Gary beat on Jonathan's shoulder, grinning savagely. "I knew it!" he whispered. "I knew he'd do it!"

Ralon was staring at Alanna, gasping for words. "*What* did you say?" he finally squeaked.

"Liar. Sneak. Coward. Bully." She threw the words at him. "You disgrace your name. D'you want me to write it down for you? Oh—I forgot. You can't read, either."

"Shut up!" Ralon screamed, his eyes bulging. "You pig! You wouldn't be so brave if your friends weren't here to do your fighting—"

"I fight my own battles!" she snapped. "I want satisfaction for all I've taken from you. They're my witnesses."

Ralon looked at the others. "They won't step in, no matter what?" he asked slyly.

"They won't. I swear on my honor as a gentleman. You'd better swear by something else, though. You don't have any honor." She slapped him with all her strength and ducked.

Ralon swung at her, missed, and Alanna came up under his swing to ram into his chest. He yelped and grabbed her hair. She punched him twice in the stomach, hard, ignoring the pain as some hair came out of her scalp. Ralon seized her throat, choking her. She shoved her thumb into his eye, stamping hard on one of his feet at the same time. Ralon screamed in pain, breaking away. They circled each other carefully. Now Ralon knew something had changed since the last time they had fought. He was sweating heavily as he charged.

Alanna lunged forward, thrusting her hip between Ralon's legs. He stumbled. She helped him fall by throwing him over her hip. Quickly she knelt on his back, knowing better than to let him up. Twisting his arms up behind him, with one hand, she used her other hand to pull his head up by the hair.

"Give up?" she panted. Ralon, gasping, nodded. She stood up, and he leaped at her, landing a wild punch on her cheek. Thanks to the dishonorable George, Alanna was ready for this. She slammed a fist up and under, into his stomach again, knocking the breath from his body. Swiftly she broke his nose with the other hand. Ralon collapsed, crying like a small child.

Alanna stood back, heaving as she fought for breath. She wiped sweat from her eyes. "Never touch me again. If you do, I swear—I swear by Mithros and the Goddess—I'll kill you." Ralon lay there, still crying.

Alanna turned to her friends. "Let's go wash."

Ralon called out, "Alan of Trebond!"

Alanna turned back to look. Her enemy was on his feet. He was a bloody mess with crazy eyes. "I'll make you pay for this!" he screamed. "Just wait— I'll make you sorry!"

Raoul clapped Alanna on the shoulder. "Come on," he said. "It's getting windy in here."

∽

*M*yles found her alone in her room, sitting in the dark. "You weren't at dinner tonight," the knight commented. Alanna blinked at him with surprise as he lit a candle.

"Ralon of Malven has left Court," Myles went on, sitting in her only chair. "Your servant Coram is bragging to his fellow Guardsmen that he knew you could do it all along. The other boys want to celebrate—they think you're a hero. Isn't that what you wanted?"

She splashed cold water on her face. "Is it? I don't know." She rubbed her face dry and looked at him. "I threw up after," she confessed. "I hate myself. I just knew more than Ralon did. And he always loses his temper when he fights—I took advantage of that. I'm as bad as he was."

"I doubt Ralon ever threw up after he beat someone smaller and younger than he was."

Alanna frowned. "You think so?"

"I'm sure of it." Myles nodded. "Alan, there will come a time when you, a knight, will have to fight someone less well trained than you. It can't be helped, and it doesn't make you a bully. It just means you learn to use your skills wisely."

Alanna thought about this. At last she sighed and shook her head. It was too much just then.

Myles ruffled her hair. "So now you've proved you're a warrior to the whole palace. Surely you want to celebrate."

Alanna made a face. No matter what Myles said, she had used fancy tricks to beat Ralon, that was all. She was still a girl masquerading as a boy, and sometimes she doubted that she would ever believe herself to be as good as the stupidest, clumsiest male.

The door opened. "Sir Myles. You beat me here." It was Prince Jonathan. "How's Alan?"

Myles stood. "I think he's tired. Alan, I'm going, but I wish you'd think about what I said."

"I always think about the things you tell me," she admitted. She gave him her hand. "Thanks, Sir Myles."

The knight bowed to Jonathan and left. The Prince looked at Alanna. "What was that about?"

Alanna shrugged. "I think we were talking about what makes a bully."

"A bully fights people littler and weaker than he is because he thinks it's fun," Jonathan said flatly. "Did you enjoy fighting Ralon? We'll forget for now he's older than you and a squire."

"When we were actually *fighting*—maybe," she replied slowly. "After—no."

"You won't find anyone smaller than you are, so you can't beat on them," the older boy said practically. "And after today we're all going to think twice about whether you're the weakest. Look, young Trebond—what did you think studying to be a knight was about?"

Suddenly Alanna felt much better. "Thanks, Highness." She grinned. "Thanks a lot."

He put a hand on her shoulder. "You may have noticed my friends call me Jonathan, or Jon."

Alanna looked up at him, not sure what was going on. "And am *I* your friend, Highness?"

"I do believe you are," he told her quietly. "I'd like you to be." He offered her his hand.

She took it. "Then I am—Jonathan."

four

Death in the Palace

Duke Gareth's lecture the day after Alanna fought Ralon was long and impressive. He spoke to her about the duty one noble owes another noble, about keeping the peace on the palace grounds and about people who became bullies. He informed her that fighting with the hands was an undignified pastime taken up by commoners, or an art practiced by Shang warriors—and that she was neither a commoner nor a Shang warrior. She had to make a formal, written apology to Ralon's father, and she was restricted to the palace for two months.

Alanna stood at attention, listening. She loved the way the Duke talked. She knew he was pleased that she had beaten Ralon, not angry. She also knew he could never tell her so, because she had broken the rules, and that she had to take her punishment without complaint, because she had known the rules when she broke them. Alanna's world was governed by rules, with a rule to cover every situation. Fighting a fellow noble in the palace was breaking the rules, and Gareth had to teach her that. Yet the rules governing what a noble could take in the way of insults said that Alanna *had* to fight Ralon, and Duke Gareth was proud of her because she had protected her honor as a noble.

Once you know the rules, she thought as she listened to the Duke with one ear, *life is pretty simple. I don't get mad at Duke Gareth because I know he has to obey the rules just as I do, and I know he isn't truly angry with me anyway. Maybe our Code of Chivalry isn't such a bad thing.*

On the second day of the eight-day-long Midwinter Festival, King Roald made Gary, Alex, Raoul and several of the other fourteen-year-old pages into squires. Each squire was placed in a knight's service. They still waited on table, but afterward they took their meals in the squire's hall. If they were needed, they also served the nobles during the evening parties, when the pages were dismissed. Alanna helped her friends move to their new quarters—rooms connected to those of the knights they now served—and wondered how big a change this would bring to her life.

Things changed, and they didn't change. The squires joined Alanna and Jonathan in what little free time they had, but Alanna missed them during the classes she had with the other pages. There was no more Gary to make wicked jokes in Deportment, and no more Alex to explain the snarls of mathematics.

Then one night Jonathan came by her room with his book on battle histories. He'd gladly help her with mathematics, he explained with a grin, if she'd show him how the battles that were so dull in the book were fought. He'd noticed in class that her way of explaining them made them seem real and interesting.

Alanna was more than happy to accept her new friend's offer. Many evenings after that they could be found in each other's rooms, their heads bent over a map or a piece of paper.

∽

The Sweating Fever struck in March without warning. It spared no one: people in the city, palace servants, priests, even the Queen. Duke Gareth was next, and the Lord Provost. Sir Myles stayed healthy. "There's so much wine in me that I don't have room for any sickness," he told Alanna. "So now will you stop telling me not to drink anymore?"

Alanna herself was fine. She was working harder than she ever had before; each time another servant got sick, her chores increased. There were no classes; most of her teachers had the sickness. Instead Alanna made beds, washed dishes, cleaned the stables. She had been taught from birth that no job was too dirty for a true noble. Now the theory was put into practice.

The pages and squires—the youngest, healthiest people in the palace and the city—were the last to fall ill. It was then that the Dark God came to the palace to take his pick of fever victims. In the city, where the sickness had started, so many had died that the Dark God's priests took the dead away in cartloads. Within a week, the God of Death had claimed three pages, five squires and the Lord Chamberlain. Raoul was the first of Alanna's close friends to get sick. When Alanna stopped for a visit, he grinned weakly at her.

"I feel silly, lying in bed when I should be working," he confessed. He shivered beneath his heavy blankets. "How are you? And how's old Coram?"

"We're both fine." She tucked the covers more firmly around him.

"And Jon?"

"Not even a sniffle. He stays a lot with the King."

"I don't blame him. Mithros willing, the Queen will get well." He let Alanna wipe his sweating face before giving her a shove. "Get out of here, before you catch it."

Alanna found then that she couldn't sleep because she couldn't forget Maude's warning to use her Gift for healing. She knew the gods punished people for ignoring magical abilities. Yet the thought of using sorcery gave her the shakes. She and Thom each had more magic than anyone she had ever known, and she knew if she used her magic and lost control of it, she would destroy herself and anyone who was nearby. Thom liked that sort of power—she didn't. She was never sure of her control over her Gift.

Gary, Francis and Alex got the fever within two days of each other. Francis was the sickest, delirious by the end of the first day. The palace healers could do nothing. Alanna overheard one of them saying that those stricken so badly the first day usually died. And there were more frightening stories— stories that the Sweating Sickness was caused by sorcery, that it drained the healers of their healing magic until they were too weak to help anyone.

Alanna had just fallen asleep one night when Coram woke her. His news was bad—Francis had just passed into the hands of the Dark God.

Alanna hurried down to the chapel dedicated to the god of death. Jonathan was already there, waiting with his friend's body. Alanna knelt in the back, not wanting to disturb the Prince. She shook as she looked at Francis lying on the altar. He might still be alive if she had done something.

Alanna was ashamed of herself.

Sir Myles knelt beside her. His hair and beard were mussed from sleep. "I'm sorry, Alan," he murmured. "I know you and Francis were friends."

Alanna looked at the knight. He was her friend and he was an adult—he would understand moral questions. And she trusted his opinion.

"Can I talk with you a moment?" she whispered. "Outside?"

They left quietly. Myles settled onto a bench just outside the chapel door. "What's on your mind?" he asked, motioning for her to take a seat.

Alanna remained standing. "Sir—if a person has power—something that can be used for good or evil, either way—should they use it?"

He looked at her shrewdly. "A power such as magic?"

Alanna scuffed a foot against the floor.

"Well—yes. The Gift."

Myles frowned. "It depends on the person, Alan. The Gift is simply an ability. Not all of us have it, just as not all of us are quick-witted or have good reflexes. Magic isn't good or evil by itself. I believe you should only use it when you are absolutely certain your cause is just. Does that help?"

Alanna tugged her ear thoughtfully. "You couldn't give a person a yes or a no, could you?"

Myles shook his head. "Not in this case. Moral issues rarely have yes or no answers."

The door opened, and Jonathan came out. "Alan?" he asked softly. He was very pale, and his eyes were bright with held-back tears.

"Thanks, Sir Myles," Alanna said. She went to her friend.

They buried Francis the next day. Raoul and Gary, finally getting better, came. The healer attending Alex was able to tell Alanna that he, too, was healing. Jonathan was at the funeral with his father. They disappeared afterward, and Alanna hurried back to her chores. She struggled with her thoughts, wondering if she should go to the healers and offer to help. She couldn't do anything for Francis now, but there were others.

The fever itself made the decision for her. Coram and Timon found her washing dishes in the kitchens the next morning.

"Alan," Timon called.

She looked up from a tubful of pots, frowning.

Coram's voice was gentle. "Th' Prince took sick last night. He's callin' for ye."

Alanna put down her dishcloth. Her throat was tight with fear. "How is he?"

"Bad," Timon said.

Alanna raced to Jonathan's rooms, the two servants behind her. Opening the door, she froze. She couldn't believe the scene before her. People were crowding around Jonathan's bed. The incense in the air made her sneeze. The priests of the Dark God were chanting prayers for the dying while the Chief Healer stood aside. Duke Baird was a beaten man. Jonathan was hallucinating already, and the healer had learned the people stricken badly from the first always died.

Fury made Alanna gasp for breath. How could anyone get well in a menagerie? How could Jonathan breathe? This went against all the commonsense rules Maude had taught her for healing: clean air, quiet, absolute cleanliness, calm and reassuring voices. Didn't these city people know *any-thing*? Alanna opened her mouth—then closed it hard. She had almost ordered these adults to get out! She could guess how they'd greet such an order from a page.

She turned to Coram. "Get Sir Myles. Now."

The burly soldier looked down at her. He knew that forward thrust of her chin. "Ye aren't plannin' somethin' foolish, are ye?"

"No more foolish than *this*." She jerked her head at the crowded room.

Coram sighed and met Timon's puzzled look. "Sh—he's Trebond," he explained. "Stubborn as pigs, all of them. We'd best fetch Sir Myles."

Alanna went outside and closed the door. She would wait in the hall rather than watch the insanity going on inside. It fortunately wasn't long before the two men returned with a very curious Myles.

"I need your help," Alanna told the knight abruptly. "Take a look inside."

Myles peered into Jonathan's room. When he closed the door, his eyebrows were raised. "You know there isn't much hope," he told Alanna softly. "Not if he's so ill this soon."

Her eyes and her voice were as hard as stone. "Maybe there is and maybe there isn't. Look—I've been keeping something back. I have the Gift, and I'm trained to heal. The village woman taught me everything she knew." When he didn't laugh, she plowed on. "I may be only eleven, but some things even an idiot knows. You don't make a lot of noise and fog the air with incense in a sickroom, Myles!

And *my* Gift hasn't been drained, like the palace healers'." She saw the doubt in the man's eyes and added, "Jonathan's been calling for me. I think he senses I can help."

Myles tugged at his beard. "I see. And what do you want *me* to do?"

Alanna drew a deep breath. "Get those people out of there. They'll listen to you." She couldn't say how she knew the people in Jonathan's room would obey a minor knight—she just knew. "Get them out of there so we can air the room, and so I can talk to Duke Baird."

"That's a tall order." Myles thought it over, then shrugged. "You're very convincing, Alan. And what have we got to lose?"

She looked at him, her eyes filled with pain. "Jonathan," she whispered.

That decided him. "Very well." He nodded to Timon. "Announce me."

Timon, looking as if his world had turned upside down, opened the door.

"Sir Myles of Olau!"

The crowd hushed and faced the door. The priests stopped chanting. Myles stepped into the room, flanked by Coram and Timon. Alanna— ignored—followed. The change in Myles was stunning. The short, stout knight was suddenly very regal and very angry.

"Have you left your senses?" he demanded. His gentle voice was sharp and clear. "No one can tell me his Majesty knows of this—this folly. I won't believe it."

No one spoke.

"Get out," Myles ordered. "This is a sickroom, not a funeral." He glanced at the priests. "For shame. The boy isn't dead yet."

After a moment the head priest bowed his head and led his followers from the room. Some of the courtiers looked at Duke Baird: *he* was supposed to be in charge. The healer nodded at Myles, relief on his tired face.

"You can do nothing here," he told the other nobles. "Myles is right. Go to your gods and pray for our Prince. It is the only way we can help him now."

Slowly they left. Only Duke Baird stayed. Alanna hurried to Jonathan's side. Her friend was stark white and sweating heavily. Alanna tucked the blankets firmly around Jon's body.

"Coram," she called. "Open the windows. Let's get some clean air in here."

Baird looked at Myles suspiciously. "What goes on here?"

"Alan asked me to help him," the knight replied. "I follow his orders."

Baird gaped at him. "*You* follow the orders of a *page?*"

"Alan," Myles said, "you owe Duke Baird an explanation."

Alanna rose and went to the healer. Quickly she

told him everything she had told Myles, stopping only to motion for Coram to close the shutters again. "I'm not grown up and as fully trained as you," she finished. "But I haven't had all my power drained, either. And he's my friend."

"Friendship will not be enough," Baird told her. "As a healer, you know normal healing takes only a little of the healer's strength. This fever doesn't. It will take all your strength—and if you *continue* to try and heal, the draining will kill you. Three of my healers are already dead. Can you risk your life against this sorcery?"

"Then you *do* believe the illness is caused by magic," Myles said.

The healer rubbed his eyes. "Of course. No one outside the city has this sickness. No natural fever will slay a healer. And I find it very interesting that only *after* all the palace healers have been drained of their power does the heir to the kingdom fall ill."

"Can none of our sorcerers fight this fever or track it to its source?" Myles asked.

"There's no one in Tortall with the power. Duke Roger could, but he is in Carthak. The King sent for him, but not even Roger of Conté can travel so far in less than a month."

Alanna listened to this and watched Jonathan. He was flushed and tossing under his blankets. She bit her lip. In a way she had caused Francis's death. She had denied her healing Gift, and he had died. She couldn't make that mistake again.

"I'll try anyway," she said. Looking at Baird's stern face, she added, "With your permission."

Baird held a hand out to her, and Alanna took it. "I'm very tired," the Chief Healer said. "If you are as able as you claim, it will be easy for you to strengthen me. Do so."

Alanna looked at the Duke's hand. Slowly, carefully, she reached inside herself. It was there: a purple, tiny ball of fire that grew as she nudged it with her mind. Her nose started to itch, as it always did when she first called on her magic. She ignored the annoyance. Her eyes watered. She gently drew the fire up through her body and let it flow down her arm into Duke Baird. He hissed, his hand tightening on hers. Alanna let the purple fire slide into the man until he could hold no more. She whispered, "So mote it be," and broke their grip.

Alanna staggered, feeling a little dizzy. Myles gripped her arm.

"I'm all right," she told her friend, then looked at Duke Baird. "I *had* to master that one. My brother always gets tired when we're hiking."

The healer was staring at her as he rubbed his hand. "Mithros guide you," he whispered. "I think the Prince actually has a chance."

He hurried from the room. Myles, Coram and Timon stared at Alanna, awed because the Duke had been so awed. Alanna felt dazed and a little lonely. She didn't like people looking at her as if she were something frightening.

"You'll stay?" she asked them, pleading.

Myles put an arm around her shoulders. "You may count on us," he said. The other two nodded.

Alanna bit her lip, thinking. "We'll try the natural remedies first," she decided. "Coram, let's build this fire as high as it will go and keep it that way." The servingman bowed and left. Alanna went to the desk and seized paper and pen. She wrote quickly. "Timon, I need these things from the kitchens and some extra blankets."

The man took the list and was gone. Myles began to build up the fire with the wood that was in the hearth basket.

"Alan?" Jonathan's voice was a deep rasp. Alanna went to him and took his hand.

"I'm here, Highness. It's Alan."

Jonathan smiled. "I know you won't let me die."

"You're not going to die," Myles said over Alanna's shoulder. "Don't even think of it."

Jonathan frowned. "Myles? You're here?" He looked around. "I dreamed there were people—"

"There were," Alanna assured him. "Myles threw them out."

The Prince grinned. "I wish I could've seen that."

"Come on," Alanna said. "You've got to sleep."

From the look in his eyes, Jonathan was ready to ask more questions, so Alanna reached for her magic once again. Stroking Jonathan's temples, she held his eyes with hers.

"Sleep now, Jonathan." Her rough, boyish voice was strangely compelling. Myles caught himself yawning. "Sleep." Jonathan thought he was drowning in violets. He slept.

Coram came with armfuls of firewood. Timon returned with blankets and the kitchen items on Alanna's list. She sent him for bricks while she settled down before the fire. Carefully she brewed mead, honey, herbs and lemon juice into a syrup for Jonathan's cough. Her hand shook as she stirred. Myles noticed and took the spoon from her.

"What's wrong?" he asked, stirring the mixture himself. "You've been shaking since you got Jonathan to sleep."

She sat down wearily. "Duke Baird was right." She accepted the glass of wine Coram poured for her and drank it down. "That fever. It takes it out of me—like nothing I've ever felt before." She sighed. "Myles? Could you talk to the King and Queen? They'll be worried—"

The knight handed his spoon over to Coram. "Say no more," he told her. He left, trying to smooth his shaggy hair.

Coram watched her as he stirred. "I hope ye know what ye're doin'."

Alanna rubbed her already aching head. "So do I."

When Timon brought in the bricks, Coram heated them in the fire and wrapped them in cloth. Alanna packed them at Jonathan's sides. Then she and Timon piled more blankets on top of the Prince. Soon Jonathan was sweating. Hard coughs tore from his chest. Alanna let her syrup cool just a little, then tipped some down Jonathan's throat.

Every two hours they changed the sweat-soaked sheets and packed Jonathan in freshly warmed bricks and blankets. The room was stifling. Their clothes stuck to their bodies—Coram and Timon both stripped off their shirts. When Myles returned, he nearly fainted from the heat.

"Duke Baird's with the Queen," he reassured Alanna. "He'll see to it that she's kept calm and doesn't come here. And pirates have been attacking Port Caynn. His Majesty is in the War Chamber and cannot leave. They both have to trust Duke Baird's judgment and leave us alone."

Alanna looked around. Three sweat-soaked men—and outside this room, the entire palace—watched her, waiting for what she would say next. It was frightening. Was it possible adults weren't as assured and as powerful as she had always believed?

She didn't have time to worry about that now. "Timon, let Sir Myles spell you," she said. "You need to rest and eat."

Timon obeyed. Now Myles helped her and Coram rewrap Jonathan, and Myles held the Prince while Alanna gave him her syrup. When Timon returned, she made Coram get some rest. By late afternoon Jonathan was coughing up the stuff that was choking his lungs. By dark he was sleeping, but his fever continued to rise. Alanna sent the others away to rest and eat while she watched her friend. Duke Baird looked in briefly and left—it was his third such visit, and he never said anything. Alanna only nodded to him. She had no energy left for conversation.

Myles returned with a tray of food. "Eat," he ordered. "And I'm setting up a cot in Jonathan's dressing room. It's your turn to rest."

Alanna knew her friend was right. She ate and then lay down in the dressing room, falling asleep immediately and not awakening until nightfall. While her friends went for a snack and a walk, she sat with Jonathan. The room was suffocating with heat, but the Prince was shivering. Sweat ran down his face. Alanna watched and gathered her strength. If the Dark God wanted Jonathan's life, he had better be ready to fight for it.

The door opened. Alanna jumped to her feet, bowing deeply as the King and Queen came into the room. She felt sorry for them. The King, who was always smiling, looked worried. Deep lines seemed permanently carved around his mouth. He kept one arm around his lady, supporting her weight. Queen Lianne sank into the chair Alanna pulled up for her. She was still not over her own bout with the fever, and her gown hung loosely on her.

"Alan of Trebond." The King kept his deep voice quiet. "How is my son?"

Alanna swallowed nervously. "As well as can be expected, sire. He slept most of the day."

Lianne's voice was kind, but a little sharp. "How can you help him? You're only a boy, no matter what Baird says."

"Your Majesty, even *I* know better than to dirty the air with incense and surround Jonathan with wailing people," Alanna told her. "Besides—he called for me. He trusts me, and he doesn't even *know* I have the Gift."

"Have you ever been trained?" King Roald asked.

"I learned all our village healing woman had to teach me, sire. I can heal, and—I can conjure. My brother's the same, only he can see people's minds and sometimes the future. I can't."

"Why didn't you tell Duke Gareth this when you first arrived?" the King demanded. "Why didn't your father tell us?"

She scuffed her foot along the floor. "My mother died having Thom and me. She had the Gift too. Father was angry—he thought their magics should've saved her. So he said he wouldn't ever use his Gift again, and we weren't to use ours. We weren't even to be taught how to use it; but Maude, the village healer, taught us in secret." She hung her head. "As to the other, I want to be a knight. Using my Gift doesn't seem fair, somehow. It's as if I'm fighting dirty." Roald nodded, understanding. "But Maude said I should use my Gift for healing. She said I had the power to heal more than most people. She said if I didn't heal, I wouldn't make up for the killing I did as a knight. I didn't listen to her." Alanna's voice was soft. "I disobeyed her, and one of my friends died."

The King put his hand on her shoulder. "You did what you thought was right, Alan. We can't all see the future, and we can't know what will be asked of us." He rubbed his forehead. "*I* should have listened to Roger," he said, more to himself than to the Queen or to Alanna. "If he were here now, teaching you boys—" He drew a deep breath and looked at Alanna once more. "Jonathan has the Gift. He gets it from me—from the Conté line.

"If—*when* he gets well, I shall see to it you lads are properly trained. I have ignored this part of our heritage, too. Like your father, I thought our magic would vanish if I ignored it." The King shook his head. "A knight must develop *all* his abilities, to the fullest. And evil is often armed with sorcery."

Alanna thought she knew what the King meant. If she had been more thoroughly trained, she wouldn't feel so helpless now. If the fever was magical, she was going into the fight badly prepared.

Lianne was fanning herself. "It's so hot in here," she complained.

"We're trying to sweat the fever out, Majesty," Alanna explained. "It's best to try all the natural cures first."

The King patted the Queen's hand. "Remember what Duke Baird said. We can trust Myles and Alan. We *must* trust them."

Lianne went to the sleeping Jonathan, taking his hand. Her eyes were bright with tears. "He's all we have, Alan. I can't—I am unable to bear any more children." She smiled bravely at the King. "If my lord trusts you, then so do I."

"Mother?" Jonathan's voice was no more than a whisper. "Father?"

Alanna hid in the dressing room. It was not long before Roald called her back. "He is asleep. Will you call us if—" The King could not say it. Impulsively Alanna reached out and patted his arm.

"We'll let you know right away if anything changes, sire," she promised.

Myles stepped quietly into the room, bowing to his king and queen. "He'll be all right," the knight told Lianne. "He has all our prayers."

"Except for those of the one who sent this fever," replied the Queen.

The King and Myles exchanged a look. The Queen was right. Who was Jonathan's enemy?

Gently the King took his lady's arm. "Come, my dear," he said softly. "We must leave."

Coram and Timon came back as Jonathan's parents left. Alanna rolled up her sleeves. "Let's get this fire built up again," she said grimly.

It was a long night. Jonathan's coughing finally stopped. Alanna listened to his chest, smiling when she could hear him breathing easily. But the fever continued, drying Jon's lips till they cracked and bled. He fought Alanna and Myles, dreaming, living through ugly nightmares. His voice was worn down to nothing, and it shook Alanna to see him scream without making a sound.

Myles grabbed her shoulders. "Alan, this can't continue! Your Gift! Use it!"

"I've *been* using it!" she cried. "And I haven't the training—"

"Go inside yourself, then! Can't you see he's dying?"

Alanna looked at the fire. It roared hungrily in the hearth, waiting for her. She rubbed her eyes. Already she was tired from the little spells and charms she had used during the day.

She picked up the last packet of herbs. It contained vervain. She had known all along it would come to this. She opened it dully, staring at the brittle leaves inside.

"Coram. Timon." Her voice sounded dead. "You'd better leave."

Coram stepped forward. "Lad—" he began worriedly. He looked at her face and sighed. "Let's go, Timon," he said. "We don't want to be here when they start foolin' with serious magic." They left, and Myles bolted the door.

Alanna threw the vervain onto the fire. She had no business trying magic like this. She was no sorcerer, and sorcerers far older and stronger than she had failed to master the forces she now sought to call upon.

A moan from the bed reminded her of why she was there. Kneeling before the flames, she whispered the words Maude told her would call the Greater Powers—the gods. Slowly, very slowly, because she was tired, the flames turned violet. She reached both hands into the purple fire.

Her essence, the stuff that made her Alanna, streamed out through her palms. She was dissolving into the fire; she was the fire. Then she uttered the spell Maude told her to use only when nothing else was left.

"Dark Goddess, Great Mother, show me the way. Open the gates to me. Guide me, Mother of mountains and mares—"

The fire roared up with a sound like a thunderclap. Alanna's body jerked, but she couldn't move away from the hearth. The fire filled her eyes. She saw countless gates and doors opening in front of her. Suddenly—there it was: the city, the city carved in black, glassy stone, the one she had seen in Maude's fireplace. The sun beat down on her. She was very warm. The city called to her, its beautiful towers and shining streets singing in her brain.

The city vanished. Now raw energy rammed through Alanna's arms, into her body. She choked back a gasp as her flesh turned into purple fire contained only by her skin. She glowed; she shimmered; she burned with raw magic. It hurt. Every part of her screamed for cold and dark to put out the fire. She couldn't hold it. She would burst like a rotten fruit.

A voice spoke, and Alanna screamed. That voice was never meant for human ears. *"Call him back,"* it chimed. *"I am here. Call him back."*

Tears ran down her cheeks. The voice and the pain were killing her. The fire was eating her alive, like a tiger.

Something inside her rebelled. She clenched her fists and fought the pain. She ground her teeth together. *She* would ride this tiger. Her body had never given the orders before—she could not let it start now. *Am I a silly child?* she thought angrily. *Or am I a warrior?*

She fought back, shoving the pain away until she had it under control. Now *she* ruled the power she had pulled from the flames. *She* rode the tiger. She was a warrior!

Alanna walked to the bed. Myles got out of her way. He had watched, helpless, when Alan screamed as he turned a bright, sparkling amethyst. The color had dimmed, but Alan continued to shine with a pale purple fire. Myles sensed that if he touched Alan now, he would be burned to death.

Alanna stood beside the bed, looking down at Jonathan. He seemed so far away, so far from her. *"He has traveled a long way,"* the terrible voice said. *"Take his hands. Call him back."*

A small part of Alanna realized that the voice

was female. "Thank you," she whispered.

She took Jonathan's hands carefully. Her mind reached into his unseeing eyes.

"Jonathan," Alanna called. "It's time to come home. Jon."

Myles stared. He did not hear a boy-child calling the Prince. He heard a woman's voice, speaking from eternities away. Awed by a power he could not understand, the knight moved even farther away from the bed.

Alanna fell into the blue depths of her friend's eyes. She was twisting in a black, writhing well. The alien place pulsed around her, enclosing her like a living thing. Shrieks and cackling and the screams of doomed souls sounded all around her. She was on the edge, between the world of the living and the Underworld. She drifted between Life and Death.

"Jon," she called steadily, feeling the power in her shoving the ugliness back. "Jon." At last she could see him. He was far below her, near the bottom of the well, near Death. A huge, dark shadow shaped like a hooded man came between them. Even in her strange state Alanna was afraid. This must be the Dark God, the Master of all death.

It was crazy to argue with a god, but he was between her and her friend. "Excuse me," she said politely. "But you can't have him. Not yet. He's going to come back with me."

The shadowy hands reached for her. Alanna

stood still, her mind sending up a shield of purple fire. "You can't have him," she said more firmly.

The shadow hands passed through her shield and held her by the shoulders. Alanna felt as if unseen eyes were looking her over. The great dark head nodded—and the shadow was gone. The Dark God had vanished.

Alanna reached out to Jonathan. Their hands clasped. "Come back," she told her friend. "This place isn't for us. Come home."

Jonathan smiled. "I'm coming." His voice was that of the man he would be one day, deep and even, calm and commanding. Did he hear a woman when she spoke? Did he think it was her? "I'm with you, my friend. Time to leave."

Their gripped hands glowed white-hot, melting the shadows around them. Their combined Gifts burned away the walls of that unreal place. At the end of the well, drawing nearer and nearer, was the room they had left so long before. Slowly the violet fire ebbed from Alanna's body. By the time they were in Jon's bedchamber, her skin was filled with nothing but Alanna—much to her relief.

"Thank you," the man in him said. He released her hand. She was Alan the page, sitting on the bed beside Prince Jonathan. His eyes were clear. He sighed and closed them. "It's good to be back," he whispered, and slept.

Swaying, Alanna stood. Myles finally dared to come close to her. He had watched the two boys burn with a steadily brighter purple light. He had heard a man's voice and a woman's voice coming from Jonathan and Alan. It was something he could never forget.

"Alan?"

She turned. "He's all right," she murmured, stumbling. "He'll sleep—" Her bones ached. Her head throbbed, and she could barely stand. "Myles?" she gasped, and fell to the floor in a dead faint.

five

The Second Year

*B*ecause she slept for three days, Alanna avoided most of the questions about her part in Jonathan's cure. When asked about it later, she gave all the credit to Sir Myles. Whenever the knight tried to discuss what had happened that night, Alanna always changed the subject. She knew Myles watched her, but she said nothing, knowing it would only bring the whole discussion up again.

Prince Jonathan also watched her. Yet he never spoke of that night. The less said about the whole thing, the happier Alanna felt. She wondered sometimes if Jonathan even remembered the place between Life and Death. It was possible that he didn't—and he never brought the subject up.

The chilly winter turned at last into spring. Alanna unpacked her light clothing once again. She dressed one morning in a fever of excitement. It was the day the pages were to go on the long-promised trip to Port Caynn, and Alanna was barely able to hold still. Suddenly she froze before her long mirror. Watching the glass closely, she bounced up and down.

Her chest moved. It wasn't much, but she had definitely jiggled. Over the winter her breasts had gotten larger.

"Coram!" she yelled, her eyes stinging with tears of fury.

The man stumbled into her chamber, bleary-eyed. "What is it now?" he said with a yawn.

Alanna stepped behind her dressing screen, tearing off her shirt. "Get to the healers, quick, and find some bandage for me—yards of it. Make any excuse you like, but get it!"

The puzzled Coram returned within minutes and shoved a bundle of white linen over the top of the screen. Alanna grabbed it and wrapped it tight around her chest.

"Ye're turnin' into a woman, aren't ye?" he asked from the other side of the screen.

"No!" she exclaimed.

"Lass, it's hardly somethin' ye c'n change. Ye're born with it—"

Alanna stepped from behind the screen. Her eyes were red and swollen. If she had been crying, Coram knew better than to mention it. "Maybe I was born that way, but I don't have to put up with it!"

He looked at her with alarm. "Lass, ye've got to accept who ye are," he protested. "Ye can be a woman and still be a warrior."

"I hate it!" she yelled, losing her temper. "People will think I'm soft and silly!"

"Ye're hardly soft," he replied sharply. "And th' only time ye're silly is when we talk like this."

Alanna took deep breaths. "I'm going to finish what I set out to do," she informed him quietly.

He put a hand on her shoulder. "Alanna, child, ye'll be happy only when ye learn t' live with who ye are." She had no answer for this, but he didn't expect one. "I'll pick up more bandagin' when I go down t' the city today," he said. "Get along now. Ye'll be late, else."

❧

$\mathcal{I}$t wasn't easy to live with the binding on her chest. For one thing, her growing breasts hurt, though luckily they remained quite small. She was twice as careful now about how far she opened her shirt, and that summer the boys tried their best to get her to take it off entirely. The best time for this was when they went swimming. All summer Alanna refused to go into the water, no matter what persuasion was used. Persuasion always stopped short of trying to physically force her—no one had forgotten Ralon of Malven.

One day near the beginning of August Raoul tried his luck. "C'mon, Alan," he teased. "One small dip. Or are you afraid you'll wash off a protective coat of dirt?"

Alanna had had enough. She jumped up, her face beet red. "I hate swimming!" she yelled. "And I'm cool enough—so lay off!"

Someone giggled. Raoul was head and shoulders taller than the page who was glaring at him so fiercely.

"Alan, he's only teasing," Alex called.

"I'm tired of being teased!" she snapped. "All summer long I put up with this. Why can't I do what I want without being pestered all the time?"

Raoul shrugged. Unlike Alanna, Raoul had no temper to speak of. Nothing seemed to make him angry. "Well, if you're going to be touchy, I won't bother you anymore."

"Fine!" She glared at the other boys. "And unless I stink, I don't want to hear about it ever again!"

There was a heavy silence. At last Jonathan said, "Come back in the water, Raoul. You can't argue with Alan—he's crazy."

Shaking slightly, Alanna returned to her shady tree. She felt more than a little ashamed of herself and wished—not for the first time—that she could keep a rein on her temper.

The boys left her alone for the rest of the afternoon. As they rode home, Alanna trotted Chubby ahead so she could catch up with Raoul.

"Raoul?" she asked softly. "A word with you?"

They dropped to the back of the column. "Are you going to yell at me again?" Raoul asked frankly.

Alanna blushed and looked at her saddle. "No. I wanted to apologize. I shouldn't have lost my temper."

Raoul grinned. "I *was* teasing you," he admitted. "Sure, you got mad. You've a right to do as you want."

She looked at him with shock. "I do?"

Raoul frowned. "I hadn't meant to say anything, but since I have the chance—Alan, you seem to think we won't like you unless you do things just like everyone else. Have you ever thought we might like you because you're different?"

Alanna stared at him. Was he teasing her again?

Raoul smiled. "We're your friends, Alan. Stop thinking we're going to jump on you for the least little thing."

"Hey, Raoul," someone called from up front. "Will you settle this bet?"

Nodding to Alanna, the big squire urged his horse to the front of the column.

"Did you patch that up?" Gary asked. Alanna turned. The other large squire was just behind her.

"Don't you know it's rude to eavesdrop?" she asked crossly.

He grinned. "How would I learn anything if I didn't eavesdrop? Listen—I'm tired of all the arguments. I'll make sure no one asks you to swim again."

Alanna hung her head. "I don't mean to be difficult," she muttered.

Gary laughed. "Of course you do. It's one of your charms. Come on. We're lagging behind."

She followed as he urged his horse through one

of the many palace gates. Between Gary and Raoul, Alanna had much to think about. The idea that she might be liked because she was different was poppycock, of course. Being squires certainly made Gary and Raoul say strange things.

She and Gary caught up with Jonathan after stabling their horses. There was a sizable group of pack mules and horses in the stableyard, waiting to be fed and cared for.

"Looks like we have an important guest," Jonathan noted. "Let's nip by the entry hall and see who's here."

The three boys hurried through the palace corridors, coming at last to the entry hall. A huge pile of baggage stood there, growing smaller as an army of servants took pieces of it away. A big man, still wearing a dusty traveling cloak, directed the palace servants and his own people.

Jonathan gave a glad cry. "Roger!" He ran to hug the newcomer while Alanna and Gary halted nearby.

So this is Jon's cousin, Alanna thought, looking the newcomer over. Duke Roger of Conté was over six feet in height, with brown-black hair and a beard neatly trimmed to frame his handsome face. His eyes were a bright, riveting blue. He had a straight, perfectly carved nose; his mouth was red and full. His white, flashing smile was filled with charm and confidence. He was broad-shouldered and muscular, with strong-looking hands. *Very attractive,* Alanna decided. *So why am I not attracted to him? If anything, I think I dislike him!*

"So he's arrived at last," she murmured to Gary. She'd have to figure out why she didn't like Jonathan's cousin later.

"I—er—'happened to overhear'—"

"You eavesdropped again," Alanna said sternly.

"As I was saying, I happened to overhear that he's to teach you Gifted ones sorcery," Gary went on. "Also, the King wants him to find out who sent us the Sweating Sickness—not that they'll try something like that again, not with Duke Roger here. Every sorcerer in the Eastern Lands would think twice before taking him on."

"He's that good?" Alanna asked thoughtfully.

"He's that good."

Duke Roger was coming toward them, one arm around Jonathan's shoulders. "So you're going to train your Gift? I'll enjoy teaching you, Cousin!" He held a hand out to Gary. "Young Gareth of Naxen, isn't it? You've grown since I saw you last."

Gary shook the older man's hand heartily. "Everyone says that, sir. Even my father says it, and he sees me nearly every day."

Roger chuckled at this. "I don't doubt your father's right." His voice was a light tenor, the most musical voice Alanna had ever heard in her life. She was staring at the Duke without shame when he turned to her. "And this young one? I'd remember eyes—and hair—like yours, I'm sure."

"Duke Roger of Conté, may I present Alan of Trebond?" Jonathan said formally.

"Trebond?" the Duke smiled as Alanna bowed. "I've heard of your father. He's a noted scholar, is he not?"

Alanna was quivering all over—*like a nervous horse*, she chided herself. She linked her hands behind her back before answering, "I believe so, your Grace."

"Oh, please!" he protested. "Just 'Lord Roger' is fine, and I'd do away with that, if I didn't think it would shock Duke Gareth. 'Your Grace' makes me feel old."

Jonathan expected one of Alan's pert answers and looked expectantly at his friend. To his surprise Alan looked thoughtful rather than charmed.

"How long are you here, Cousin?" Jonathan asked, drawing attention away from Alan's odd silence.

"My uncle says he wants me to stay here for a while," Roger replied, looking down at the Prince. "'Make your home with us' was the phrase he used." The Duke shrugged his wide shoulders. "I think my wandering days are over."

Jonathan grinned. "I can't see why you've been avoiding us, anyway."

"Not avoiding you," Roger corrected him. "Educating myself. The difference is considerable. Now, would you be so kind as to take me to their Majesties? I think it's time I greeted them."

Alanna watched the Prince and his cousin go, frowning. She shook herself, trying to shed a cloak of uneasiness.

Gary looked at her. "Are you falling sick with something, youngster?"

Alanna hunched her shoulders impatiently. "I've never been sick in my life."

"Then what's wrong? He was being friendly, and if you were a dog your hackles would've been up."

"I'm not a dog," she said crossly. "Why should he be friendly with *me*? I've never seen him before."

"But he'll have heard of you. You helped heal Jon—*now* what?" There was a strange look in Alan's eyes. If Gary hadn't known his friend better, he'd have sworn that look was one of fear.

"I don't like grownups taking an interest in me," Alanna replied. She *was* afraid. "I don't like people nosing in my affairs, especially sorcerers. Come on—we'll be late for dinner."

Gary followed, more confused than ever by Alan's response. Was he hiding something? It was a question for him to ponder on a rainy day.

∾

Shortly after Roger's arrival, each page or squire was summoned to an interview with the King's nephew: he tested them all for the Gift. Gossip said he would find it even if a boy tried to hide it.

Alanna was one of the last to be called.

Clenching sweaty hands, she entered Duke Roger's study. The Duke of Conté was lazing in a tall-backed chair, turning a jeweled wizard's rod between his fingers. He glimmered in a many-colored tunic and red-purple hose; if Alanna admired anything about him, it was Roger's taste in clothes.

He smiled. "Alan of Trebond." He gestured to the chair facing his desk. "Please, have a seat."

Alanna sat carefully, folding her hands in her lap. Every nerve in her body was on the alert. She hadn't gotten this far to be caught.

"I understand you used your Gift to heal my cousin of the Sweating Sickness."

"Sir Myles directed me, sir."

"It must have required a good deal of power on your part, though. You took a great risk."

"My village healing woman had trained me, sir. And I *was* exhausted for days after." She watched his face. He seemed to accept that Myles had done the thinking and she had supplied the power, so Myles hadn't talked about that night. She liked that.

"Well, at least I don't have to ask you any use-less questions. We already know you have the Gift, and in abundance. And you learned from your vil-lage healing woman?"

"Yes, sir. My father didn't know we were trained, though. He didn't want us learning any sorcery—he'd throw a fit if he thought I was learn-ing it here."

"Then we won't tell him. You say 'we.' Tell me

about your brother. I understand you're twins?" Roger's bright eyes never left hers. Alanna frowned and rubbed her forehead. Suddenly she had a headache.

"He's in the City of the Gods, sir. Father sent him to be a priest, but I think he plans to take up sorcery."

Roger smiled. "A noteworthy ambition. What is his name?"

"Thom, sir." Why was he staring at her so?

The man looked at the jeweled rod in his hands. "My cousin speaks highly of you, Alan of Trebond."

"We're friends, your Grace." She discovered she couldn't look away from him.

"My uncle-in-law, Duke Gareth, also speaks highly of you. You are a most worthy young man by all accounts."

Alanna blushed with shame. If they knew the truth, they wouldn't speak well of her. "Your Grace is very kind." She wished he would let her go. She had never had such a fierce headache.

Roger sighed. Suddenly Alanna could look away from him, and the pain in her head lessened. "I am not often kind, Alan." He tapped his rod against his hand for a moment. Finally he said, "I think I learned what I needed to. Report to me in my solarium Monday after breakfast. You may go."

Alanna bowed and left gratefully, her head still pounding. She felt exhausted and a little nauseous. Coram appeared at her side, a worried frown on his face.

"Well?" he demanded.

Alanna didn't ask how he knew. It was almost impossible to keep anything from the palace servants.

She rubbed her temples. "Maybe I'm crazy—but why do I feel like more went on in there than just his asking me questions?"

"Because maybe it did." Coram pulled her into an empty room. "I heard the Duke of Conté can catch yer will and make it his own," the man whispered. "They say he'll reach into yer mind, make ye say what he wants t' hear—unless ye're defended. Unless there's a wall in ye he can't reach over."

"Well, I don't know that kind of magic," she snapped, the headache making her cross. "But he didn't learn anything from me I didn't want to tell him. I'm sure of it."

"Then yer magic's stronger than his," Coram said. "Or ye're protected by the gods."

This was too much for Alanna. She laughed and gave Coram a shove. "You've been nipping at Cook's wine! Protection from the gods! Making me say what I don't want to say! Go on with you!"

Coram opened the door. "Laugh if ye want." He shrugged. "I'm only an ignorant old freeman, listenin' to stories by the fire. But if it's all so funny, why do ye look as if someone pulled ye through a currycomb?"

There was no answer to that, and Alanna didn't even try to invent one.

⌇

*O*ne fall evening Stefan the hostler gave her a note.

"*You've been looking for a horse,*" it read. "*I have one. Come to the city first chance you get. George.*"

A horse! A real horse, the kind of horse a warrior ought to have! Alanna scribbled sums on a sheet of paper. After careful figuring she decided she *could* buy a horse—if it was the *right* horse. Wistfully she said farewell to sweets for a long time—but a real horse would be worth it. She was tired of riding palace horses, and Chubby was getting old. The pony deserved a rest.

She knew very little about horse buying. With such a large purchase, Alanna wanted an expert opinion. Who could she ask? With wrestling in the afternoons as her worst subject, it meant she could take free time only in the morning. Coram had guard duty in the morning, so that let him out. Also, Coram didn't know about George, and Alanna didn't want him to know. For some reason, she suspected the old soldier would not approve of the thief. Gary was also unavailable—he was restricted to the palace for one of his numerous pranks.

She nibbled her thumb. Who could she introduce to George?

⌇

*A*lanna needed two steps to match one of

Jonathan's. This made the walk into the city brisk, but their pace was suited to the crisp fall day. Alanna watched her friend, thinking. The Prince, just fifteen in August, was growing again. Already he measured five feet seven inches. His voice was beginning to boom and crack, too, just as Gary's and Raoul's had last year. Soon Alanna would have to start faking the voice change herself. *We're all growing up,* she thought, and sighed.

Jonathan heard the sigh and looked down at her. "I'm glad to help pick your horse," he commented, "but why all the secrecy? You never told me you had relatives in the city."

Alanna made a face. "I had to tell Duke Gareth *some*thing. You see, the man we're meeting—he's not a relative. He's a friend. Thanks for coming with me, Jonathan."

He tousled her hair. "I'd do anything to get out of Reports in Council. It's the spring planting today—that always puts me to sleep."

Alanna led him into the Dancing Dove. Old Solom was asleep on one of his tables. Alanna roused him with a friendly slap on the back.

"Wake up, you old drunk. Is George around?"

Solom peered at her. "Why, it's Master Alan. But not Master Gary?"

"Master Gary won't be around till Midwinter Festival," she told him.

"At his tricks again, eh?" Solom shook his white head with appreciation. "He be a lively one. I'll get his Majesty." He hobbled up the stairs.

Jonathan was looking around. "'His Majesty'?" he whispered. "And how does this man know Gary?"

"Oh, Gary comes with me all the time." Alanna avoided the other question by following Solom. Jonathan had no choice but to go along.

George was finishing breakfast when the innkeeper showed them in. Staring at Jonathan, he rose. Finally he bowed, his grin mocking. "Solom, go back to sleep," he ordered. When the older man was out of earshot, the thief murmured, "Your Highness—I'm honored." He looked sharply at Alanna. "And it seems I've misjudged you once again, youngling. I'll not do that a third time, be assured."

Alanna turned pink. "I just brought him along for fun," she muttered.

"What's going on?" Jonathan wanted to know, fixing Alanna with a bright eye.

"You didn't tell him?" George asked.

Alanna shook her head. "Prince Jonathan, this is my friend, George."

"Alan's not tellin' you that my work doesn't always mean stayin' right with the law," George explained. "But come, lads. You'll be wantin' to see the beast."

He led them down another stair to a door that opened behind the inn. Seeing Alanna's curious look, George said, "It pays to have at least two doors—even three." He pointed to the roof. Two shuttered windows looked out over the roof of the one-story kitchen. A ladder was even placed against the kitchen wall to make it easier to reach George's rooms.

"Aren't you worried about thieves?" Jonathan asked. When his companions broke out laughing, the Prince frowned thoughtfully.

"So Gary kissed Lady Roxanne?" George inquired. "I'd've kissed a sweeter armful, myself."

"It was a bet," Alanna explained.

"For ten nobles, I'd still have kissed someone prettier," George replied.

"How'd you know about that bet?" Jonathan wanted to know. "It was a secret."

"I've friends in the palace," George said. "There isn't much you can keep from your servants, Highness."

Jonathan opened his mouth to ask something else, but Alanna distracted George with a burst of questions about her friends at the Dancing Dove. So the Prince kept quiet through the short walk, thinking an idea through.

They turned into a small alley. George stopped and unlocked a tall gate. They entered a stableyard, George locking the gate behind them.

Alanna gasped. Her eye had been caught by a beautiful young mare. The horse's coat was gold, offset by a flowing white mane and tail. Gently Alanna caressed the mare's nose. The creature whickered softly, rubbing against her hand.

"George, she's the most wonderful thing I've ever seen." Suddenly Alanna remembered this might not be the horse George had in mind. "George—she *is* the one you brought me to see?"

George bit back a smile, seeing the dismay in Alan's violet eyes. "Aye, lad, she's the one."

"She's perfect." Alanna and the mare watched each other, spellbound.

Jonathan stepped into the stall. He ran expert hands over the mare's legs and shoulders, petting her absently. Finally he looked at George.

"She's stolen," he accused.

George dug his hands into his breeches' pockets, grinning. "Highness, would I do such a thing?"

"I hope you didn't steal her, George," Alanna murmured.

"I've a bill of sale. *I* don't balk at stealin' a proper horse, young sprout, but I knew you would." George handed a paper to Jonathan, who examined it carefully.

"It's legal," the Prince said at last, returning it to George.

"How much, George?" Alanna wanted to know.

The thief looked at the page, his hazel eyes guarded. "Eight for the mare, two for the tack—ten gold nobles and she's yours." His tone dared Jon to argue. The Prince didn't take the dare.

Alanna never hesitated, although it was the largest amount she had paid in her life. She counted the money into her friend's hand and returned to admiring the horse—*her* horse. "We're going a long way, you and I," she whispered to the mare. The horse butted her gently, as if agreeing.

George took down a plain leather saddle and bridle. "Here you go."

"George, if you ever want my life, you can have it," Alanna said quietly, meaning every word. "What's her name?"

"She hasn't one. The Bazhir who sold her didn't dare name such a noble lady."

"I'll call her Moonlight. D'you like that, girl?"

The mare tossed her head. Alanna laughed and set to work saddling her horse.

Jonathan drew George away from the stall. "That's not a third of what you paid for that mare."

George's voice was low. "Would you have me deny the lad his heart's desire? He's been riding that pony all year when the poor beast should be at pasture and Alan on a horse. That care-for-naught he calls Father will never get him a proper mount. Call it a birthday gift, if you will. I'd give her to the boy outright, if he'd take her."

Jonathan grinned ruefully. He had had his own experience with his small friend's pride. "I can't let you take a loss of at least twenty gold nobles. Besides—I owe Alan my life." He looked sharply at the man. "I suppose you know about that, too."

"I may," the thief admitted.

Jonathan drew a sapphire ring off his finger.

"That should more than cover the price of the mare."

George turned the gem over in his long fingers. "It does indeed," he said slowly, and made a rapid decision. "You've no proper horse of your own, I hear. Not a chief mount, a horse you'll ride above all others. You might have an eye to this." He opened a closed stall. Inside stood a great stallion, as black as Jonathan's hair. "The ring would also cover *his* price, Highness. I don't take charity."

Jon hesitated, biting his lip. "Are you trying to buy me off, King of the Thieves?"

George smiled. "If the lad didn't tell you, how'd you guess?"

"I sit on my father's Council, remember. I've heard about you."

George smoothed a hand over the stallion's nose. "I've no wish to buy your silence. This is a sale, right and straight. When I bought the mare, I couldn't let this one go. The dealer was a filthy old Bazhir. These two in his string were like gems in garbage. I figured the lad would want the mare, and I can always find a buyer for this fellow."

Jonathan examined the stallion. He was more restless than Moonlight, but he quieted under the Prince's firm hand. "You have an eye for horseflesh, George."

"I like horses," the man admitted. "I've a chestnut mare of my own, as pretty as you please. I'd be flattered if you'd have a look at her, sometime."

"I'd like that." Jonathan looked at George

thoughtfully. Suddenly he smiled and offered his hand. "Thank you. A good horse can mean a man's life."

George took the offered hand, his eyes searching Jon's for hidden motives. "You honor my taste, Highness."

"I'm Jonathan—to my friends. Kings and princes should be friendly, don't you agree?"

George laughed, but there was respect in his gaze. "I agree—Jonathan. And never fear I'll use that friendship. My game of wits is with my Lord Provost—no one else."

"I hope so"—Jon grinned—"or Alan, Gary and I are in a lot of trouble."

"George," Alanna said. The other two looked at her. Her face was bewildered. "I—I don't understand," she stammered. "Why do this for me? You went to a lot of trouble. Why?"

George looked at her for a long moment. Finally he replied, "And why do you find it so hard to think someone might like you and want to do things for you? That's the way of friendship, lad."

Alanna shook her head. "But I haven't done anything for you."

"That's not how it works," the thief said dryly.

This was confusing, and Alanna said so. George laughed and took them to lunch.

～

Shortly after this the four youngest pages—Alanna, a new boy named Geoffrey of Meron,

Douglass of Veldine and Sacherell of Wellam—
were ordered to one of the indoor practice courts,
instead of the staff yards. Awaiting them were Duke
Gareth, Coram and Captain Aram Sklaw, head of
the Palace Guard. The Captain, a hard-bitten old
mercenary with a patch over his missing eye,
looked the boys over.

"Hmph!" he snorted. "Not a promising one in
the lot!" He pointed a thick finger at Geoffrey.
"You—you look like a dreamer to me. Blood makes
you sick, eh? You'd rather read than fight. Huh!" He
eyed Douglass. "Aye, you like your food, don't you?
Hang around the kitchens, I wager, begging from
Cook." He squinted at Alanna. "You? You're not big
enough for bird feed. You won't be able even to lift
a sword, let along swing it." Alanna started to argue
and remembered Duke Gareth's presence. She
stored that remark for later—she'd show Sklaw!
The mercenary turned to Sacherell. "I've seen you
on the courts. Lazy, that's what you are, and slow to
boot." He stood at attention before the Duke. "With
your Grace's permission, I'd like to be excused."

Duke Gareth's smile did not quite fit under the
hand he used to hid it. "You ask to be excused every
time, Aram, and yet you manage to turn out cred-
itable swordsmen—every time." He looked at the
boys, his thin face stern once more. "You are going
to learn the art of fencing." Alanna gulped with
alarm—Duke Gareth always made her nervous.
"No, don't look at me like that, Alan—I don't waste
my time on beginners. I don't have enough for the

more promising students as it is. Captain Sklaw and Guardsman Smythesson will be your teachers. You'll learn how to forge a sword, how to draw it, how to hold it. For the next few months you'll eat, sleep and study with your sword on. If it leaves your side, you get an overnight vigil in the Sun's Chapel. This is not wrestling or tilting. You might go all your lives without wrestling, when you are knights. However, you may safely bet you'll have to defend yourself—or someone else—with a sword at least once before you die. If any of you give the Guardsman or the Captain cause to complain, you'll talk to me. I know how much you boys enjoy our little chats." The Duke nodded to the men. "Gentlemen, they're yours." He walked from the room.

Sklaw looked at them and snorted. "Before you likely-looking lads touch a blade, you'll make one. Guardsman Smythesson will instruct you there, poor man. I leave them to you," he told Coram, and walked out after the Duke.

Coram sighed, his face grim. "Well, lads—let's be off to the forge."

It was the beginning of a long, hard winter. After the practice swords were made to Coram's satisfaction, Sklaw took over. He instructed them in the stances and passes that were such an important part of fencing. He taught them how to get a sword from its sheath quickly—a feat that looked much easier than it was. Always Sklaw hovered nearby, criticizing, growling, complaining. The boys learned to do everything while wearing their practice swords, because there was no telling where Sklaw would turn up. The only place it was safe to take the blade off was in one's room, when one was bathing—and even then the door had to be locked. Alanna made sure her door was locked.

Sklaw singled her out for special treatment, perhaps because she was the smallest of the group. She did nothing right, or even better than last time. She was clumsy; she was lazy; she didn't practice because where were her muscles? She was a midget; she had been dropped on her head at birth; she would never be a full-fledged knight, only a "Lord," fit to do nothing but sit at home and write poetry. Alanna took the abuse and practiced doggedly, trying to deafen herself to the old villain's talk.

"How d'you expect me to be confident if you're bellowing at me all the time about how bad I am!" she yelled at him once.

Sklaw grinned without humor. "Well, laddie, if you've let an old buzzard like me hurt your confidence, you couldn't have had much in the first place."

Alanna bit her lip rather than answer him back, after that.

Spring came, and Duke Gareth returned to their class.

"We're trying something new today, girls," the Guard Captain growled as the Duke of Naxen took a seat. He tossed two sets of padded practice armor at Geoffrey and Douglass. "Meron. Veldine. Let's see if you can use what you've learned on the move."

The two boys put on the padding and assumed the "guard" position. "Begin!" Sklaw barked.

After a few moments Alanna closed her eyes. She had seen Duke Gareth fencing with Alex, who was the best swordsman among the squires. This was a mockery of that kind of fencing. Geoffrey would lurch forward and swing his sword at Douglass. Douglass would hurry to block the swing, stumble back, then lurch forward to try a swing at Geoffrey. After a while Duke Gareth called a halt. Between them, he and Sklaw went over the duel, showing each boy how he could place his feet better, how he could move quickly without stumbling, how he could improve his balance. Finally they were permitted to strip off their now sweat-soaked padding.

"Wellam. Trebond." Sklaw shoved two fresh suits of padding at them. "If you can do as well, I'll be much surprised."

Alanna assumed the "guard" position, feeling her knees trembling. It was like taking any other kind of test, only ten times worse. A knight lived or died by his swordsmanship. Without a mastery of swordplay, she would be no knight, have no great adventures. Suddenly Sacherell, who was a friend and a sometimes companion, looked like a menacing ogre—a tall, bulky, menacing ogre.

"Begin!" Sklaw ordered. Alanna stumbled backward as she tried to avoid Sacherell's lunge. Recovering her balance, she brought her sword up just in time to block Sacherell's down-coming swing. She stumbled again and recovered only in time to block another swing—and another—and another. She stumbled and blocked, without making any swings of her own and without really getting her footing. The boy lunged forward suddenly, his sword point headed straight for Alanna's throat. She tripped and fell over her own feet, dropping her sword. When she looked up, Sacherell was standing over her, his sword in the "kill" position at her throat. She closed her eyes as Sklaw let out a full-throated roar of laughter.

∽

That night she lay awake, staring at the ceiling. Over and over she "fought" the duel with Sacherell in her mind. What had gone wrong?

She heard Coram moving around in his room, getting ready to take up the predawn watch. When he left the chambers, she went with him, a small, silent shadow. Wordlessly she accompanied him down to the kitchens, sitting beside him as he flirted with a sleepy scullery maid and ate his breakfast. Still silent, she followed him up to his post on the castle walls. Together they watched the sky over the Royal Forest go from gray to red-orange as dawn came.

At last Coram remarked, "Sleep at all?"

Alanna shook her head.

"I've seen worse."

"You were there?"

"Aye."

Alanna closed her eyes and shivered. The humiliation for Coram would have been terrible, and that made her own humiliation worse. It was bad enough to look like an idiot in front of her friends and Duke Gareth. But Coram was the man who had taught her how to use a dagger as a weapon, to shoot an arrow, to ride her pony. Coram had encouraged her all this way, had made himself a wall between her and the people who might have discovered who she really was. She had failed Coram, and he had seen it.

"I don't understand it," she whispered finally. "It—it was like—my body wouldn't do anything I told it to. My mind was saying, 'Do this! Do that! Do something!' And my body just wasn't connected. Sacherell—"

"Sacherell was well enough." Coram yawned. "He's a bit of a natural. Ye're just not a natural with a sword, Master Alan. Some are born to it, like me. I never knew aught else, and I never wanted to. Now, some—some never learn the sword at all, and they don't survive their first real fight. And then there's some—"

"Yes?" Alanna asked, grasping at this straw. She was obviously not born to the sword, and she had no plans for dying in her first fight.

"Some *learn* the sword. They work all the extra minutes they have. They don't let a piece of metal—or Aram Sklaw—beat them."

Alanna stared at the forest and thought this over. "It's possible to *learn* to be natural?"

"It's just as possible as it is for a lass t' learn t' beat a lad, and the lad bigger and older than she is, and in a fair fight. Well—*ye* fought fair."

It had taken weeks of training in secret to beat Ralon. The long hours, the bruises and her constant exhaustion were fresh in her mind. *But it was worth it*, Alanna thought. *More than worth it.*

She stretched, yawning widely. "Can I borrow your sword?"

Coram looked at the weapon hanging from his belt. "This? It's bigger than ye are!"

"Exactly."

Coram stared at her for a moment, then slowly unbuckled his belt. He handed the sword to Alanna, his face expressionless.

Alanna hefted the weapon in her hand. It was the largest, heaviest sword she had ever handled. It would be work to wield it with only one hand. "Thanks. I'll return it later."

She trotted off to find an empty practice room with plenty of mirrors. Coram was right. A sword could not beat her—and neither could Aram Sklaw.

six

Womanhood

*I*t was the fifth of May. Alanna awoke at dawn,
ready for another session with Coram's big sword.
She got out of bed—and gasped in horror to find
her thighs and sheets smeared with blood. She
washed herself in a panic and bundled the sheets
down the privy. What was going on? She was bleeding, and she *had* to see a healer; but who? She
couldn't trust the palace healers. They were men
and the bleeding came from a secret place between
her legs. Hunting frantically, she found some bandage and used it to stop the red flow. Her hands
shook. Her whole body was icy with fear. The servants would be coming to wake the pages soon. She
had to do something in a hurry!

She gnawed her thumb until it bled. Coram
was on guard duty. Besides—she couldn't tell him.
This wasn't something she could confide to the old
soldier.

She could trust only one person to help and
keep quiet. There were those who might wonder
just how trustworthy the King of Thieves could
be—Alanna wasn't one of them.

With no time to waste, she couldn't afford to sneak from the palace and run all the way to the city. She would have to ride and take the consequences. A quick word to Stefan, and Moonlight was saddled. The hostler even lured a guard away from one of the smaller gates. Alanna rode out for the city at a full gallop. Within minutes she was hitching her mare to a post behind the Dancing Dove.

Swiftly she clambered onto the kitchen roof and pried one of George's shutters open. George himself had taught her how to make a second-story entry. When Alanna slid into the man's room, she was seized from behind. A very sharp knife pressed against her throat.

"Didn't your mother ever teach you to enter by way of the door?" a voice drawled softly.

Alanna held very still. That knife was no joke. "George—it's me! Alan!"

The man let her go and made her face him. He wasn't dressed—he always slept bare. "So it is." He put his knife on the table. A smile lit his eyes. "And what makes a noble sprout break into the Rogue's bedroom?"

"I need your help." She twisted her hands together. "I've got to see a healing woman right away."

"A healin' woman, is it? You'll have to give me more than that, lad." George crossed his arms over his chest, waiting. He had always known there was a secret to Alan. "Why a woman? And why a city healer? The best in the land are at the palace."

Alanna swallowed hard. "I'm not a boy." It was incredibly hard to say. "I'm a girl."

"You're a—you're a *what!*" George yelled.

"Hush! D'you want everyone to hear?" She scuffed her boot against the floor. "I thought you'd guess. You have the Gift."

"And *your* Gift shields you. Alan, if this is a jest, it's a poor time for one."

She glared at him. "D'you want me to take my clothes off?"

"No—great Mithros. Turn around whilst I get clothed."

She obeyed, arguing, "That's silly. I've seen you naked before."

George hunted for his breeches. "This is different. All right—turn about. Why d'you need a woman?"

Her eyes were pleading. "Don't ask. Please."

The thief made a face. "Come on, then." He hustled her down his back stair and into the street. "I know just the lady—she was a priestess in the Temple of the Mother here in the City before she married, got trained there. She's my own mother. She wouldn't talk if you pried her jaws apart." He spotted Moonlight waiting patiently. "You're little enough—the mare will carry us both." He swung himself into the saddle behind Alanna. "We're ridin' for the Street of the Willows."

Alanna nodded and urged her horse forward. George's warmth at her back was oddly comforting.

"What's wrong?" he asked again.

"If I knew, I wouldn't be so damned scared," she snapped.

"That's true—I've never seen you overset," he said thoughtfully. "We've got to talk, you and I." They turned down a small street lined with walled houses. George dismounted and unlocked a gate marked with the healer's sign—a wooden cup—circled once in red and once in brown. "What are you called, then?"

She hesitated. "If I tell, you might forget and let it slip out later."

"Not me, youngling." He motioned for Alanna to ride into the courtyard and then closed the gate. "I let nothing slip."

She dismounted. Moonlight butted her affectionately. "It's Alanna," she whispered.

George's mother came to the door of the house. She was a tall woman, with her son's twinkling hazel eyes and an air of command. Only a single streak of white in her chestnut hair revealed her to be a little more than middle-aged.

"A patient for you, Mother," the thief announced. "I'll be stabling the mare."

Mistress Cooper showed Alanna into a small, neat room. Healing plants of all kinds hung from the rafters, giving the room a fragrant smell. A small wooden table covered with a clean sheet sat in the room's center.

"Sit there," Mistress Cooper ordered. "Now. What's the problem?"

Alanna explained quickly that she was a female, not a male, and that she was a page in the palace. Mistress Cooper raised her eyebrows, but said nothing. Alanna drew a breath and added, "I—I'm bleeding."

"Bleeding?" was the calm response. "Where?"

Red with embarrassment, Alanna pointed. George's mother began to smile. "Has it happened before?" Alanna shook her head. "Did you injure yourself there? No? When did it start—this morning? No pain?"

Too ashamed to speak, Alanna either shook her head or nodded, depending on the question. There were others so personal she wanted to hide when she thought about them. Her embarrassment only tripled when Mistress Cooper began to laugh.

"You poor child," she chuckled. "Did no one ever tell you of a woman's monthly cycle? The fertility cycle?"

Alanna stared. Maude had mentioned something, once—

"That's what this is? It's *normal?*"

The woman nodded. "It happens to us all. We can't bear children until it begins."

"How long do I have to put up with this?" Alanna gritted.

"Until you are too old to bear children. It's as

normal as the full moon is, and it happens just as often. You may as well get used to it."

"No!" Alanna cried, jumping to her feet. "I won't let it!"

Again Mistress Cooper raised her eyebrows. "You're a female, child, no matter what clothing you wear. You must become accustomed to that."

"Why?" Alanna demanded. "I have the Gift. I'll change it! I'll—"

"Nonsense!" the woman snapped. "You cannot use your Gift to change what the gods have willed for you, and you would be foolish to try! The gods willed you to be female and small and redheaded, and obviously silly as well—"

"I am not silly!" Alanna wailed. "I just—" She rubbed the back of her hand against burning eyes. She knew Mistress Cooper was right. She had tried to use her Gift once to make herself grow, and her head had ached for days.

"Well, then, perhaps not silly." A comforting hand was laid on Alanna's shoulder. "Listen to me. Your place in life you can always change, whether you have the Gift or not. But you cannot change what the gods have made you. The sooner you accept that, the happier you will be." She led Alanna into the kitchen and put a tea kettle on the fire. "You're not used to your body doing things you haven't asked of it, are you?"

Alanna made a face. "It's bad enough my chest keeps growing. Now something like this happens."

She put her head in her hands. Finally she looked up and said, "What do I have to know about this—this thing?"

"Your cycle comes once a month, and lasts five days or so. Bathe each day. Bandage yourself, of course. The cycle will not come if you lie with a man and he gets you with child." The woman made a cup of tea and handed it to the girl. "Here. This will make you feel better."

Sipping it did make Alanna feel calmer. "Will it slow me down?"

"Not so long as you stay out of men's beds. A babe will certainly slow you down."

Alanna shook her head. "I don't plan on children."

"Many girls don't." Mistress Cooper poured herself some tea. "Do you know what happens when you lie with a man?"

Alanna blushed. "Of course."

The woman smiled. "You know the man's side of it, I see. Well, a woman enjoys it too, and one time is enough for you to get with child." She looked at Alanna carefully. "I'll give you a charm against your getting pregnant, then. If you change your mind, you can throw it away."

"Pigs might fly," the girl muttered.

The look in Mistress Cooper's eyes was skeptical. "We'll see. Now—George will have a few questions. Shall I bring him in? It's best he knows all." Alanna nodded. The woman opened the kitchen door, calling, "Stop listening at keyholes, my son."

George walked in and lounged against the kitchen table, looking anxiously at Alanna. "All's well then?"

"She'll be fine," his mother replied. "Tea?"

"Is it that calming tea of yours? Gods know I need it. So, youngling—the truth, now."

Alanna told them everything. "I can't stop now," she finished. "I didn't ask to be born a girl. It's not fair."

George waved an impatient hand. "Hush your nonsense," he ordered. "Bein' a girl hasn't slowed you down yet. And surely you don't plan to stay a pretty young man all your life?"

"No, of course not. I'll tell them the truth when I'm eighteen and I have my shield." She sighed. "If they hate me—well—I'll have proved I can be a knight, won't I? I'll go into the world and have adventures. They needn't ever see me again."

George raised his eyebrows. "I haven't heard such foolishness in all my life. Are you tellin' us Jon will hate you? Gary? Raoul? Or your friend, Sir Myles? My ears are deceivin' me!"

"But I'm a girl," she cried. "I'm *lying* to them. I'm doing men's things—"

"And you do them better than most young men," George replied firmly. "Hush yourself. Think of them hatin' you *if* it comes to be. And don't worry. Your secret is safe with us." He hugged her around the shoulders.

Alanna rested her head against his chest, her eyes filling with tears of gratitude. She blinked them away and whispered, "Thank you, George."

"I'm callin' you Alanna, when we're alone," he said. "I think you should be reminded of who you are."

Alanna remembered her monthly cycle and said bitterly, "Fat chance I have of forgetting."

Mistress Cooper chuckled, guessing what had prompted Alanna's remark.

Alanna shrugged. "I suppose you insist—"

"I do," was the calm reply.

"Just don't let it slip. I've come too far now."

"He doesn't forget details," Mistress Cooper said dryly. "He must get it from his father, for he never had it from me." She went into the room where she had first talked to Alanna.

George chucked Alanna under the chin. "I'll enjoy watchin' you grow up, lass. Count on me to help."

Alanna gripped his hand, meeting his eyes. "I never thought for a second that I couldn't."

"You're probably the only person in the city besides me who can say that," George's mother commented, returning. "He's a good boy, even if he is crooked. Here. Slip this on."

Alanna looked puzzledly at the gold symbol dangling from a thin cord. She had never seen such a letter before, and she could feel it radiating power. Quickly she slipped the cord over her head, tucking it under her shirt. The feeling of strange magic vanished.

"Let George's people bring me to you from now on," Mistress Cooper instructed. "I doubt you'll need me much, though. Give me your hand."

Alanna obeyed. The woman just touched her fingers, then pulled away as if she had been burned.

"Now what?" Alanna wanted to know.

"Poor lass." There was pity in the woman's face. "The Goddess has Her hand on you. You've been given a hard path to walk." She tried to smile. "Luck to you, Alanna of Trebond. You'll need it."

∽

*A*lanna was just slipping into her rooms when Coram found her.

"Two guesses as to who's wantin' to see ye."

Alanna made a face. "I couldn't help it. The problem was urgent."

"Yer problem now is urgent, too," was the reply. "The Duke's fit to be tied."

For visiting the city without permission, Duke Gareth restricted Alanna to the palace for two months. She also had to report to him during her time after the evening meal and run his errands. She took it without complaint, since she had no choice. She certainly couldn't tell a displeased Gareth why she had ridden off for the city.

Her thirteenth birthday passed, and it was August before she was free to leave the palace again.

Even after she was taken off restriction Alanna remained on her best behavior. The Duke of Naxen had never been satisfied with her vague excuses for her morning ride to the city, and he watched her, so she watched herself.

Duke Gareth was not the only one keeping an eye on her. Sir Myles still observed her at odd moments. Her friendship with the knight had deepened steadily, until she was spending some nights playing chess with her older friend rather than joining the Prince and his circle. For one thing, Myles told fascinating stories. Myles could also explain why people behaved as they did. Although fighting was becoming second nature to her, Alanna didn't understand people. Myles did, and she turned to him for instruction.

They were playing chess one fall evening when Myles asked, "Have you ever seen my estates? They lie just off the Great Road North, between here and Trebond."

Alanna frowned at the board. "I've never been anywhere except Trebond and Port Caynn."

Myles raised his eyebrows. "You should see more of Tortall. Did you know I have ruins up at Barony Olau dating back to the Old Ones?"

Alanna was fired with curiosity. She knew a little about the Old Ones. They had sailed across the ocean to build a civilization north of the Inland Sea. Bits and pieces were all that was left: parchments that lasted centuries, mosaics showing white cities with high towers—and ruins. The royal palace was built on the remains of one of their cities. Alanna had always wanted to know more about these people who had come before hers.

"Are they good, your ruins?" she asked eagerly. "Have you ever found anything there?"

Myles's eyes danced with amusement. "They're large, and I've found a number of things there. Would you like to ride up with me and have a look? You're in check, by the way."

"I'd love to go. D'you think it's true, that the gods were afraid the Old Ones would challenge them, so they rained fire on the Eastern Lands? There." She moved her king out of danger. She glanced at Myles in time to see an odd, thoughtful look on his face.

"I never knew you were so interested in the Old Ones—or the gods."

Alanna shrugged. "It's not something I talk about much. Duke Roger doesn't like to answer questions about the Old Ones or the gods. Well, he says we aren't old enough to understand. And the others aren't very interested."

"I don't think that's wise," Myles commented. "Our gods are much too busy in our lives for us to ignore them." He moved a piece. "Check, and mate."

Alanna was dressing for bed when Timon came for her. She changed back into her clothes rapidly and followed the servingman.

"What have ye done now?" Coram called after her. "Why does the Duke want to see ye this time?"

"How should I know?" Alanna said, turning to scowl at the soldier. "Maybe he likes my company."

Instead of taking her to Duke Gareth's office, near the King's council chambers, Timon took Alanna to the Duke of Naxen's private study, in his personal suite. Alanna was shocked to find Duke Gareth wearing a bright brocade dressing gown.

The tall man looked at her and sighed. "I suppose you know Sir Myles wants you to ride with him to Barony Olau tomorrow?"

Alanna gulped. "He mentioned my visiting him, but I didn't know it'd be today or tomorrow, saving your Grace's presence, sir." She twined her hands nervously behind her back.

The Duke smiled thinly. "I'm not angry, if that's what's making you babble. I'm simply puzzled. I wasn't aware the two of you were so close."

Alanna shifted her weight on her feet. "We play chess, sometimes," she admitted. "And I wait on him at dinner—you gave me that duty, sir."

"So I did."

"And he knows things I don't understand. I can talk to him, sir." Alanna blushed. "I didn't mean to imply—"

The man actually grinned. "Don't put your foot in it any more than you have, lad. I'm not here to be your nanny. And I'm not displeased that you and Myles are friends. It's good for you to have an older man to talk to. If your own father had any—" He stopped short. Alanna was surprised to see him blush faintly. "That was uncalled for. Forgive me, Alan."

"I know of nothing to forgive you for, sir," she said honestly.

"All right, then. You'd better get some sleep. Myles plans an early start. I'll have Coram wake you. You'll be gone for a week. I expect you to keep up with your studies, or I'll think twice about any other outings of this sort."

"Thank you, your Grace." Alanna bowed deeply and hurried from the ducal presence. She ran back to her rooms, to find Coram waiting up for her. She told him her news, hardly able to stand still from the excitement. "And the Duke wears a red-gold brocade dressing gown. Can you imagine?" she asked as she disappeared behind her dressing screen.

Coram chuckled. "It's things like that that remind me who ye are. Sometimes even I forget ye're not a lad."

Alanna, in her nightshirt, popped into bed as Coram doused the candles.

"Coram?" she said when he had settled under his own blankets.

"Aye?"

"D'you think anyone else has—guessed—that I'm not a boy?"

The man yawned. "Unlikely. Ye've taken too

much care with yer disguise. Now, go to sleep. Or at least let me get some. The dawn watch'll be the death of me."

Alanna was up, dressed and packed when Coram came for her the next morning. He handed her a roll and a glass of milk. "Drink and eat," he ordered her sternly. "Did ye get any sleep last night?"

She grinned sheepishly. "I don't think so."

"Well, behave yerself and don't gulp that milk. He won't leave without ye."

Coram was right. Myles was awaiting her in the courtyard, dressed for riding. The very thought of Myles riding made Alanna stare. Somehow she had never envisioned the older man on a horse. Then she scolded herself mentally. Myles had had to pass all the tests she did. How could he have been knighted otherwise?

She enjoyed the day-long ride to Barony Olau. Myles had plenty of stories to tell, and it was nice to forget palace discipline. The sun was beginning to sink in the west when they turned off the Great Road. Unlike Trebond, Barony Olau was no fortress built to fight off mountain bandits and raiders from Scanra. Myles's home was set in a long valley and surrounded by acres covered with brown stubble. Toward the hills Alanna could see rows of trees.

"My people are farmers," Myles explained, seeing the direction of her gaze. "Barony apples are the finest in Tortall—if I do say so myself."

"It's a lot different from Trebond," Alanna replied. She stroked Moonlight's neck—for Moonlight's comfort or her own, she wasn't sure.

The rooms Myles gave her were small and comfortable. The floors were covered with bright rugs. A fire burned in the hearth, and the windows didn't let any drafts chill the air. Alanna thought of her own home again and sighed.

The servants were polite and well spoken. When she explained her love of privacy to the man Myles sent to wait on her, he bowed and replied, "As the young master wishes." She did not know the man went immediately to Myles and relayed her wishes, or that Myles sat up very late thinking.

Over breakfast the next day Myles asked, "Are you up to the ruins? We'll have to go on foot—the ground's too uneven for horses."

She was more than eager to get started. After gulping her breakfast, Alanna rushed to change clothes. She donned thick stockings, heavy breeches, a warm shirt and a sturdy coat before pulling on her most comfortable boots. As an afterthought, she thrust a pair of gloves into her coat pocket. Alanna did not like the cold, and the days were turning crisp.

When she joined Myles, she found he was dressed like she was. "No, Ranulf," he was telling his major domo. "No servants." He chuckled. "I think you'd have trouble getting anyone to go with us."

Ranulf nodded. "You're right enough there, my

lord. You'll return before dark? I'll have even more trouble getting a search party out for you once the sun's down."

"Well before dark," the knight promised. "We're off then."

Alanna waited until they were away from the castle before asking. "Why don't your servants like the ruins?"

"My people claim they're haunted," he said. "But I doubt it. I've explored them for years without seeing a single ghost."

"Why explore them so much?"

"I'm writing a paper about the place," was the reply. "I want to show how the house was laid out, who lived there, how they lived. I'm almost finished." He tugged his beard. "I doubt many will read it, but the work gives me satisfaction."

Alanna shook her head. She was no scholar. "Why bring me here?" she asked, to change the subject.

"Because I was compelled," Myles answered.

She stopped dead. "You were *what?*"

"I was compelled," he said patiently. "For seven nights in a row I had the same dream. You and I were exploring the ruins, dressed exactly as we are now. When I asked Gareth to let you accompany me, the dreams stopped."

"Oh."

"Oh, indeed." They started forward again. "I'm an everyday man. I like my books and my brandy and my friends. I like everything in its place, and I like to know today where I'll be tomorrow. When the gods brush my life—they brush everyone's life at some point—I get nervous. There's no accounting for what the gods want."

The woods opened up, and Alanna halted. The ruins lay before them. In some places the walls were taller than she was. They were built with marble, and the stone gleamed as if it had been carved the day before. A gate made of heavy black wood dangled half off its bronze hinges.

"Shall we go in?" Myles asked. He led the way through the gates. Alanna stopped just inside, scratching her itching nose and looking around. The remains of the stone walls stretched before them in neat rows, forming buildings and rooms inside the buildings.

Myles pointed, his finger describing a large area walled by stones. "I think this was the main house. See the door?" The knight tapped a slab of black wood leaning against a wall. "It's six centuries old, at least." He moved ahead confidently. "I believe this was the kitchen," he went on as Alanna followed. "When I was younger, I found cooking implements here. I'll show them to you when we get back."

"What are they made of?" she asked.

Myles rubbed his nose. "It looks like bronze or copper, but it polishes to a higher shine than new metal. I think it's the coating they were dipped in.

The Old Ones treated everything with it—metal, wood, paper. Anything that might show age. They were terrified of aging."

Alanna stared at him. "Sir?"

"No, lad, I didn't pull that out of thin air." Myles grinned. "I can read their writing. From what I have read, they feared aging more than anything."

Alanna began to explore, keeping a sharp eye on the ground. A glint at the edge of a marble block caught her attention. It was a spearhead. She rubbed it until it shone. Looking around, she saw brackets carved in the stone blocks lying nearby. Those brackets would easily fit spears, swords, axes—

"Myles!" she called. "I think I found the armory!"

The man came over. "I agree. And you made another find." He examined the spearhead. "I'm interested in cooking gear, not weapons. You'll probably find more of these. You're a sharp fellow, Alan."

In the corner of the armory Alanna discovered a great piece of stone lying on the ground. Unlike the blocks that formed the walls, this slab was jet black. A metal handle was set in one side. Alanna rubbed it with her shirtsleeve.

"What makes you say that?" she asked, squinting at the edges of the slab.

"How many thirteen-year-old boys could come

to a place like this and figure out where the armory was?"

She tugged at the handle. The stone didn't move. "Myles, you seem to think I'm special. I'm not, really." She tugged again, with both hands this time.

"It won't move," he said. "Mithros knows I tried often enough. I think it's just the armory door."

Alanna braced her feet firmly and gripped the handle. "Maybe if you'd give me a hand—" she muttered, tugging with all her strength. Myles was coming to help her when there was a groan of mechanisms long unused. Alanna jumped out of the way as the great slab slid toward her. It uncovered a stairway, leading down into darkness.

Alanna turned, sweaty and triumphant, to find Myles looking at her oddly. "Drat it, Myles, I just put my back into it!" she cried. "Any other boy could've done it!"

"I was sixteen when I last tried to move that thing," Myles told her slowly. "I had a friend with me, one of the local lads who was my servant. He's the blacksmith now, and he was no weakling then. We couldn't budge it."

"Well—maybe there was dirt in the gears, and a rain washed it away or something," she said crossly. She started down the steps. "Aren't you coming?"

"Don't be foolish, Alan," Myles cautioned. "We don't have a torch. That tunnel could lead anywhere. You won't get far without light."

She grinned up at him. "Ah, but you forget. I *do* have light." She held up a hand, concentrating on her palm. Sweat formed on her upper lip as she felt the magic uncurl inside her. Something else uncurled in the tunnel, but she ignored it for the heat building on her palm. When she opened her eyes, her hand was glowing with a bright violet shine. "Come on," she called, trotting off down the passage.

"Alan, I order you to come back here!" Myles shouted.

"I'll be right back!" she called. She could feel a strangeness around her—no, two strangenesses. One frightened her. It was black and ghostlike, hovering just outside the light shed by her magic. The other called her with a high, singing voice she couldn't have ignored even if she wanted to. Her nose tickled, and she sneezed several times. The singing filled her mind, drowning out Myles's voice.

Her light struck something that broke it into a hundred bright fragments. She didn't notice the darkness closing in behind her as she picked up something that glittered beautifully. It was a crystal, attached to the hilt of a sword. Long and light, the blade was encased in a battered dark sheath. Alanna's hand trembled as she lifted it.

"Myles!" she shouted. "Guess what I found!"

"Get back here!" he yelled. She looked up, alarmed. There was fear in Myles's voice. "A storm's coming up—and if it's natural, I'm a priest!"

Suddenly the light of Alanna's magic went completely out. Darkness swirled around her in long tentacles that tightened on her body. She opened her mouth to scream for Myles, and no sound emerged. She fought to breathe and fought to throw her magic into the stifling blackness, but nothing happened. She tried to shove it away with her arms and legs and found the blackness had bound her tight. It was squeezing her ribs, forcing the air from her lungs. Alanna gasped for breath. The darkness filled her mouth and nose. Brilliant lights burst in her head, and she struggled like a crazy person. Nothing affected the darkness. Her struggles got weaker and weaker. She tried to fight even harder, but it was hopeless. She was dying, and she knew it.

For the first time in her life, Alanna stopped fighting. She had used up all her air, all her strength, all her magic. She was weaponless. The darkness was entering her brain, and she was dying. With an inner sigh—almost one of relief—she accepted that fact. As her knees buckled, Alanna took the knowledge of her own death and made it part of her.

The crystal on the sword blazed, its light penetrating the darkness in her brain. Suddenly the fearful grip on her body and mind relaxed. She drew in a lungful of air, shocked to find that she still could. She opened her eyes and closed them, nearly blinded by the blazing crystal.

Somewhere outside Myles was calling for her, his voice nearly drowned out by approaching thunder. Alanna used the crystal's light to guide her back to the entrance of the tunnel, feeling the blackness in full retreat before her. Still shaky, she scrambled to the surface. As she entered the upper air, the crystal went dark once more.

Alanna glanced at the sky. Black clouds boiled overhead; lightning was already striking a few leagues away. Myles seized her arm and pulled her from the tunnel entrance just as the slab ground over it once more. Alanna stared at it, wondering just what was going on. She had accepted death. Why wasn't she dead?

"No time to ponder it!" Myles yelled in her ear. "Let's go!"

They headed for the castle at a run, Myles half carrying a bewildered Alanna. The high wind whipped twigs and branches into their faces, and within moments they were drenched by the sudden onslaught of rain.

Inside the castle, Barony servants steered them to hot baths and dry clothes. Alanna bathed and changed, still not believing she was alive. Picking up the sword, she went to find her friend.

Myles was awaiting her in his morning room. A room like this would never have been found in a fortress like Trebond: the huge windows overlooking the valley were too vulnerable to enemy archers. Here at peaceful Olau, Myles could see his fields, the distant village, even the Great Road on a clear day. Now he sat in a deep chair, watching the rain streaming down the glass. A steaming pitcher and two mugs were at his side.

"Have a toddy," he said, handing a filled mug to her. "You look as if you need it." Alanna stared at the steaming liquid, trying to remember what she was supposed to do with it. "Drink up, lad," Myles urged gently. He drained his own mug and refilled it, watching her.

Alanna sat carefully in a chair, staring out the window. Finally she raised the mug to her lips and sipped. The hot liquid sent ripples of fire running through her. Perhaps she *was* alive, after all. She took another large swallow, and another.

"I thought I was dead," she said at last. "I guess not." She handed him the sword. "Here. I found this in the tunnel."

Myles examined the sword carefully without taking it from the scabbard. He ran his fingers along the sheath, rubbed the metal fittings with his thumb and squinted at a candle flame through the crystal. "What happened?" he asked as he looked the sword over.

She told him in a few brief words, watching every movement of his face.

"Is the crystal magic?" he asked finally.

"I don't know. My magic doesn't make it work. It only—it only came to life when I quit fighting to stay alive."

"I see," he murmured. "You accepted death—and the stone saved your life."

This didn't make sense to Alanna, so she ignored it. "Aren't you going to draw the blade?"

Myles looked out the window thoughtfully. "Storm's letting up," he observed.

Alanna shifted impatiently in her chair. "Well?"

"No—I'm not. You are." Myles held the sword out to her.

"I can't!" she protested. "They're your ruins. It belongs to you."

Myles shook his head. "You haven't been paying attention. I was compelled to bring you here. You opened the passage when I've tried to do it for years, and failed. Something happened down there, and the sword protected you. And don't forget the storm. I can take a hint, Alan."

"It belongs to you," she protested, almost tearfully.

"It never belonged to me." He thrust it at her. "Let's see what she looks like, lad."

Reluctantly Alanna stood and took the sword. The hilt fit her hand as if made for her. She closed her eyes and drew the sword.

Nothing happened. She glanced at Myles, embarrassed. Her friend was grinning at her.

"I feel silly," she admitted.

"After what happened this morning, I was expecting something dramatic, myself. Well?"

Alanna hefted the blade. It was thinner than a broadsword, and lighter, with a broadsword's double edge. The metal was lightweight, with a silver sheen. She lightly touched a thumb to one edge and cut herself. Grinning with delight, she tried a few passes. It felt wonderful in her hand.

"What will you call her?" Myles asked.

She didn't question Myles's calling the blade a "her." "Seeing's how it brought such a reaction from—from—"

"From whatever guards the ruins?" the knight suggested.

"I guess that was it. Anyway, seeing's how it brought on a storm and all so fast—how about 'Lightning'?"

Myles raised his mug in a toast. "To Alan and Lightning. May you never meet a better blade."

Alanna drained her own mug. "Uh—Myles?" she stammered, sliding her blade into its sheath.

"Hm?" The knight was not deceived by her innocent tone.

"I—I would rather nobody else knew about— well, what happened. Could—could we just say I picked Lightning from your armory?"

"You'll tell Jonathan, won't you?"

"Of course. But—I don't want anyone else to know. If that's all right with you."

"Certainly, lad. As you wish." Myles refilled his mug, wondering what—or who—Alan was afraid of.

∾

Alanna expected people to notice Lightning—

she would have been hurt if they hadn't. Even Duke Gareth asked about it, as did Captain Sklaw. "Not enough weight," the Captain grunted when he first lifted it. When he tested the edge, the look on his face changed to one of respect. "It'll do," he said finally. Alanna had to be content with that. Everyone accepted the idea that Lightning was a gift from Sir Myles, though Alanna told Jonathan the truth, privately. The Prince was fascinated by her experience and asked a good many questions. He even tried his own magic on Lightning, attempting to make the crystal glow. Nothing happened, and the Prince finally gave up, saying the exercise was giving him a headache.

Alanna told Coram the truth as well. She felt she owed it to her old comrade. Coram said nothing, but he would not touch the sword either.

When George asked to see Alanna's new blade, she handed it over willingly. To her surprise, the thief yelped and dropped the weapon. He made her pick it up.

"It's filled with magic, and of a kind I've never encountered," he said. "You tell me 'twas simply hangin' in Sir Myles's armory?"

Alanna opened her mouth to lie, then closed it. When she spoke, it was the true story she gave. George heard her out, shaking his head in wonder. "You *accepted* something?" he remarked. "*You?*"

"I didn't have any choice," she snapped. "I was going to die whether I wanted to or not. But when I stopped fighting it—"

"When you *accepted* it."

"Will you stop dithering about *accepting* things, George? Anyway, that's when the crystal worked. And I haven't been able to make it work since."

"Hmph. Well, I'm glad you escaped—and I'm gladder still that Lightning is strapped to your waist." George nodded at the sword. "A magic blade—whether you can work the magic or no—may well come in handy."

Someone else noticed that Lightning was not all she seemed. When Alanna walked into her sorcery class for the first time after her return from Olau, Duke Roger smiled at her. "I hear you have a new sword, young Alan. May I see it?"

Alanna hesitated. She did not *want* to hand her sword over to Duke Roger, and she had no reason on earth for feeling that way. Reluctantly she unclipped the sheath from her belt. She could feel Jonathan watching her suspiciously, wondering what was taking her so long.

"It's just a blade Sir Myles had around," she said. "I don't think—"

"I've made a lifelong study of the art of swordsmithing," Roger told her. He held out a hand. "Let's see."

Alanna gave it to him, hating him at that moment more than she had ever hated anyone. She quickly doused the emotion.

Roger froze, his eyes going wide. His face turned pale, and the knuckles of the hand gripping Lightning were white. Suddenly the air around him turned a dark, shimmering blue. Instinctively Alanna stepped forward to snatch her sword away, but the color vanished as quickly as it had appeared when the Duke carefully put the sword on the table.

"How did you get this?" He looked at her, his eyes commanding. "Speak up! How did you get it?"

Alanna turned red, and her chin stuck forward dangerously. "I got it from Sir Myles," she replied, fighting to keep hold of her temper. "I stayed with him last week, and he gave it to me."

"He—gave it to you. Just like that."

"It was in his armory—sir." Alanna could feel her shoulders getting stiff with anger. "Nobody was using it, and he knew I didn't have a sword of my own." She reached over and picked up Lightning. "By your leave, your Grace." She clipped the sword to her belt, buying time to get her rage under control.

"I see. You're certain that's the way of it? You aren't withholding some—some insignificant detail? Something you think would not interest me?" Roger's voice was quivering with—what? Rage? Impatience? Fear? Alanna wasn't sure. The Duke realized the boys of the class were staring at this break in his usual calm charm, and he tried a smile.

"Forgive me if I press you, Alan. Did you know this blade is magic?"

Alanna looked up. Her face was innocent, wide-eyed and bland. Jonathan recognized the look

Alan wore when he was about to tell his most out-
rageous lies. It was obvious to Jon that there was
something about Lightning that had shaken his
cousin Roger loose from his normal smiling self,
and that Alan did not want to tell the truth about
the sword. *Keep it simple,* the Prince thought to his
redheaded friend. *He'll spot the lie if you make it
fancy.*

Jonathan did not have to worry. "Magic, your
Grace?" Alanna was saying. "I just like the heft of it.
It's lighter than most swords, but—"

"There's magic in your sword, Alan," the Duke
interrupted patiently. Alanna hid a satisfied smile.
Roger believed her! "It is old magic—far older than
anything you've encountered, probably. That would
explain why you didn't realize immediately that the
sword is unusual. Can you make the crystal glow?
No, don't look at me as if I were raving. Try to make
the crystal glow."

Alanna made it *look* as if she was trying. She
used her Gift to bring sweat to her face and to color
the air around her light violet. She would walk to
Trebond and back before she'd try to really work
the crystal for Duke Roger! In any case, she hadn't
been able to make it work before. This time would
be no different.

"Very well," Roger said finally. "Stop. You're
only tiring yourself. The magic that could unleash
the powers in the crystal—and the sword—is lost
to us forever." This at least sounded honest, as did

the discouragement in the sorcerer's voice. "A shame. Does Sir Myles know how old the sword is? Or that it is magical in nature?"

"I don't know," Alanna hedged. "I think he does—he found it in some ruins near Barony Olau. He said the ruins belonged to the Old Ones. May I sit down now, sir?"

Roger stood, turning his jeweled rod in his fingers. "Of course. I have delayed our lesson too long as it is. Take care of that blade, Alan, if only because it is very old and very valuable. I am certain Sir Myles, noted scholar that he is, was aware of its value when he gave it to you. A mark of esteem from an estimable man." He stared off into the distance for a moment, then faced his class. "Today we begin the study of illusion. Before you learn the practice—the casting—of illusions, you must first learn the theory behind making things seem to be what they are not."

Alanna took her seat and watched the Duke of Conté recover his presence. He relaxed, and the atmosphere in the room relaxed. Once again the boys were hanging on his words with obvious delight.

Alanna, however, was not listening. Instead she fingered the crystal at Lightning's hilt, thinking about what had just happened. The Duke felt something powerful in her new sword. Moreover, he was afraid of Lightning's magic. *That* was something to remember.

Even more important, she realized, she didn't dislike the Duke of Conté—she hated him. She hated him with a deep, fierce energy she had never known she had, and she didn't have the slightest idea *why*.

∽

One snowy night Alanna was leaving her special indoor practice court after an hour with Coram's sword and an hour with Lightning when she bumped into Stefan.

"Lookin' for ye," the hostler muttered. He was nervous at being inside the palace. "George sent this along." He thrust a wad of paper into her hand and rushed back to his beloved horses.

A single sheet of paper with George's handwriting was folded around a sealed envelope. Alanna hurried to her rooms and bolted the door. Sitting on her bed, she read George's note:

"Seems your brother took you at your word when you said to send your letters through me. Here's one. —G."

Alanna broke the seal on the letter with fingers that shook. Until now the twins had only exchanged cautious notes, since Duke Gareth received all the pages' mail. Thom was a poor letter writer, in any case. This, however, was different. After learning Alanna's true identity, George had offered to smuggle letters to and from the City of the Gods. This was the first totally honest chance to communicate with each other that the twins had had in almost three years.

> *Dearest Alan,* (Thom wrote)
>
> *I'm in the Mithra cloisters now. At least I don't have to put up with giggling girls all the time. They made us shave our heads, but I suppose it'll grow back by the time I leave. We wear brown robes. Only Initiates wear orange.*
>
> *I'm glad you got someone safe to pass our letters through, even if you took your time about it. But, I suppose they keep you busy. How's Coram? Is he happy in the Palace Guard? Maude comes by every six months or so to check on me. She acts as if she were a chicken and I a duck she hatched by mistake. She says Father is working on a paper tracing the Rylkal Document. I wish him luck. He should be busy with that for the next ten years.*
>
> *We can trust this man George, can't we? I ask because it's important. A certain noble sorcerer has been asking questions up here about me. I think you know who—the one who had such an interest in your Lightning. Watch him! He has a reputation for slowing down, sometimes stopping the careers of young sorcerers who may turn out to be as good as he is. It's a warped kind of compliment—you must have him worried enough that he had to check*

and see if your twin was like you. I think he's been thrown off the track where it concerns me. I play it stupid here. It would help if you spread the word down there that your twin isn't too bright. Say I was dropped on my head, or something, when I was little. That's what my Masters believe, anyway. I know a lot more than they think I know, and I practice at night, when the others are asleep.

Enough bragging. Your friend has secrets, and he has a reputation for being dangerous. The Masters here say he's the best in the Eastern Lands, and they ought to know. Here's a piece of City of the Gods gossip you'd better think over. We heard of the Sweating Fever when it was over with, and you wrote some of the details—I wish I could've seen it! A fever caused by sorcery that drains and kills healers is a magical working you hear of once in a life- time. Everyone was, of course, naming all the living sorcerers who could be powerful enough to pull off such a thing. Only three names came up much—your smiling friend's name was one. True, you say he was in Carthak. But wouldn't a sorcerer powerful enough to strike down an entire city with a sickness be power- ful enough to do it from leagues and leagues away? And who is between him and the throne? I wouldn't want to be the Prince, not with him for my only heir.

Well, it's only a theory. Give me a few more years, and we'll give your smiling friend a run for his money. Till then, speak softly to him and let him think you like him. People who've let it be known they don't like him sometimes disappear—or die of strange diseases.

I've tried looking in on you in the fire, but you're shielded by forces I haven't encountered before. You aren't holding out on me, are you? Good luck to you. I expect we'll be hearing from each other more often now. Take care, and watch the nobleman I mentioned.

Your loving brother,
Thom.

Alanna read the letter three times, then burned it until only fine gray ash was left in her fireplace. Thom had given form to some of her worst suspicions. She wished she could discuss her feelings about Duke Roger with someone, but Jonathan and the boys worshiped him, and Alanna didn't think she had anything substantial enough to confide to Myles. She sighed and added a log to the fire. Maybe she could say something to George. It was all too complicated for one page to figure out.

As to being shielded by mysterious forces— Thom was being silly. As soon say the gods themselves were looking out for her! If Thom's mention of guardian forces dovetailed with Mistress Cooper saying the Goddess was interested in the things Alanna did, or Coram's theory that the gods had protected Alanna through Duke Roger's questioning—well, that was for Thom, Coram and Mistress Cooper to worry about. Alanna herself had enough problems.

∾

*W*inter passed quietly. Alanna occupied all her time with lessons, working every extra hour she had so she could be as good as, if not better than, the boys. Her lessons in sorcery went on week after week, with Duke Roger keeping a careful eye on his students' progress. He was very big on theory, she soon discovered, and would often spend several weeks on the ideas behind a spell before permitting them to try a spell in concrete form. It made for very slow study. Many of the spells Roger chose for them to learn were ones Alanna had already learned from Maude. Keeping Thom's words in mind, she chose not to tell Roger she already knew these spells, some of them in more advanced forms. Instead she peeked ahead in the scrolls Roger gave them to read and found herself looking at books of magic that she was supposed to leave alone. She suspected that Jonathan was deliberately locking himself into a secluded library at night and practicing more advanced spells from a reader Roger had forbidden them to touch; but Alanna chose to say nothing, either to Roger or to Jonathan. What Jon did was his business, after all. She herself never bothered to tell anyone where she disappeared to when she went to work with Coram's sword in secret.

One free morning, safe in George's rooms, Alanna caught herself trying the spell for the shielding Wall of Power that was in one of George's books. The moment she saw a wall of glittering purple fire go up around her, she shouted "So mote it be!" and broke the spell. "What am I *doing?*" she asked George in disgust.

George took her hands in his big ones. "You're doing the smart thing. Oh, you'll be a great knight and rescue ladies and slay dragons and the like, but not all the monsters you meet are dragon shaped. Remember what your brother said about Jon's smilin' cousin."

Alanna gave him look for look "Do *you* think there's danger from Duke Roger?"

George shrugged and released her hands. "I'm but a poor, uneducated city lad," he replied, his hazel eyes twinkling. "I only know if someone hands me a weapon—any weapon—and I can use it, use it I will. And think on it, Alanna. What's the line to the throne, with no children after Jonathan?"

She counted on her fingers. "The King. The Queen. Jonathan. And—and Duke Roger." She snapped her fingers in exasperation. "You and Thom are silly. If Duke Roger wants to be king so bad, and he's so all-fired powerful, why doesn't he take the throne now?"

"Because some powerful people surround it, lass," George replied. "I'd not want to have Duke Gareth for my enemy, no, nor my Lord Provost either. That quiet Sir Myles of yours bears some hard watchin'. And look at Jonathan's own friends: Gary, who's sharper than his father even; Alex, who's a rare hand with a sword; you, with your Gift; and your brother in the City. He's going to wait, our smilin' friend." George tossed an apple into the air and speared it with his dagger. He picked it up and tugged it off the blade, biting into it thoughtfully. "He'll find out who stopped Jonathan from dyin' durin' the Sweatin' Sickness. He'll make friends and sow favors. He'll take King's people and make them *his* people. He'll get rid of some who would never come to him. Then he'll strike." He pointed the dagger at her. "So learn your spells, youngling. You'll need them before your life's out. Unless I'm mistaken, the Duke of Conté doesn't like you any more than you like him."

∾

While Alanna mixed swordplay with spells—both where no one could watch her—Jonathan met the people of his city. That winter he and Alanna went down to the Dancing Dove whenever they could. Here Jon was "Johnny," the rich merchant's son George had taken a liking to. At the Dancing

Dove men didn't fall respectfully silent when Jonathan spoke. They were more likely to tell him "Ye're but a lad. Wha' d'ye know? Hush and listen t' yer elders!"

Jonathan hushed and listened. He made friends with the most dangerous thieves and murderers in the Eastern Lands. He learned to pick pockets and throw dice with ease. He flirted with flower girls and watched as thieves divided their night's haul. He was seeing life very differently from the way it was seen from the palace, and he was eager to learn all he could. No one ever guessed that the heir to the throne was sitting there, sipping a tankard of ale and occasionally tossing a set of dice.

Gary often went along, and Raoul was eventually introduced to George and his circle. Jonathan suggested Alex also be brought along, but that was the winter Duke Roger asked that Alex be his squire, until Alex's Ordeal of Knighthood. Alanna didn't even have to say that she wanted no one so close to Roger to meet George—Alex was simply too busy to spare much time for his old friends.

Winter melted into spring, and combat training among the squires reached a high level of activity. Since custom dictated that the Heir take the Ordeal if Midwinter came between his seventeenth and eighteenth birthdays, it seemed likely that Jonathan would be needing a squire that year. And since they had reached their eighteenth birthdays, Gary, Raoul and Alex would also be taking the

Ordeal of Knighthood. All three were watching the squires and the oldest pages, trying to make a choice.

Competition to be one of the favored four squires was fierce. Jonathan, of course, was the Heir, and the other three came from the noblest families of Tortall. Everyone liked the big, somewhat shy Raoul. While Gary's sharp wit and sharper tongue had made him enemies, he was also respected. Alex was Duke Roger's squire, and some of the Duke's popularity had rubbed off on him. The squires and the pages who would be made squires at Midwinter worked relentlessly, particularly when one of the four was in sight.

All, that is, except Alanna. Although she was to be made a squire that Midwinter, she did not consider herself to be in the running, and she said so. The other boys wanted to know why.

"It's easy," she explained wearily. "Look at me. I'm the shortest, skinniest boy in the palace. My wrestling is terrible, and I'm not that good a swordsman. No one will want a weakling like me for a squire."

"But you're best on horseback, especially since you got Moonlight," Douglass protested. "And you're best at archery and tilting and staff fighting and weapons. And you're a good student—all the Masters say so, behind your back. Are you saying even Jonathan won't pick you?"

Alanna made a face. More than anything she

wanted to be Jonathan's squire. "Jonathan most of all. The Heir needs the best squire the kingdom can supply. My swordsmanship's too weak, and I'm too little. Geoffrey of Meron's good. The Prince should pick him."

That was what she told her friends. She knew they didn't believe her, but she didn't care. The truth was, she didn't feel worthy of being someone's squire. She was a girl, and she was a liar. And at any moment, the truth could surface. In the meantime, the fact that she could always be beaten at wrestling and that she was only an average swordsman would do. Jonathan would pick Geoffrey or Douglass, and that would be the end of it.

～

*I*n April that changed. Lord Martin of Meron— Geoffrey's stern-faced father—rode north to visit his son and to request additional troops for his fief. Fief Meron was better known as the Great Southern Desert: leagues of sand stretching from the Coastal Hills to the Tyran Peaks. This harsh land was the home of the Bazhir, tribesmen not all loyal to the King or to his governor, Lord Martin.

The morning after Lord Martin's arrival, he conferred with the King and Duke Gareth for several hours. The King had decided that Jonathan and the boys who would soon be knights should take this chance to see what the Bazhir were like. The situation in the desert being what it was, the odds were good that each knight would fight against the Bazhir at least once in his lifetime. The squires, under the guardianship of Sir Myles and Lord Martin, would ride south with the new troops. The pages would have their own long ride later in the summer to Fief Naxen, in the east.

After this decision was made and lunch was eaten, Duke Gareth and Lord Martin went out to the fencing yards. Lord Martin had once been famed for the quality of his swordsmanship, and he and the Duke had already had one friendly match, the evening before. Now the two men took their seats at the side of the yard, prepared to see what the older pages and younger squires looked like.

"Let's see what they can do, Captain Sklaw," Duke Gareth instructed.

Sklaw looked around the yard, his one eye twinkling viciously. "Meron." Geoffrey bowed gracefully and picked up his padded cloth armor. Captain Sklaw was grinning as he pointed. "Trebond. You haven't done freestyle since that first time. Let's see you fall over your own feet again."

Alanna felt herself turning hot and cold with terror. Someone was shoving her practice padding into her hands; numbly she put it on. Sklaw was right. She hadn't fought freestyle—without each pass and move already assigned to her by Sklaw—since that awful first bout with Sacherell just a year before. She had done drill—endless repetition of the same movement—or one-on-one "plotted fighting" in which each member of the team had to make a certain set of movements dictated by Sklaw, while the other member used the countermoves Sklaw had given *him*. That sort of thing went back and forth between two duelers all afternoon, and it certainly didn't prepare anyone for freestyle dueling. In addition, she had her night practice and morning practice, but she was always alone, and it was only drill. Alanna drew deep breaths, feeling faint. Once again, here was Duke Gareth and Captain Sklaw, and Coram was clearing the boys out of the central dueling area. She slid the cloth helmet over her head and accepted a sword from Douglass. With surprise she saw it was not the practice sword she had made, but Lightning.

Even Lightning isn't going to help me now, she thought, stepping up to the mark and bowing to Geoffrey. She drew her sword and assumed the "guard" position.

"Begin!" Sklaw ordered.

Geoffrey lunged forward to attack. Alanna held her ground, blocking his down-sweeping sword with a force that jarred both their bodies. Following the "Crescent Moon" drill, she disengaged and swirled Lightning around in a half-circle, cutting for Geoffrey's side. The taller boy hurriedly blocked her and lunged back out of the way, bewilderment showing in his dreamy hazel eyes. Alanna, unthinking, followed with the second strike of the Crescent Moon, swinging Lightning back in the other direction and forcing Geoffrey to block her again, rather than attack. ("It's always better to attack than to defend," Coram had told her when they talked about fencing late at night. "Always. Ye don't win with defense—ye only hold th' other feller off, or wear him down. Attack and have done with it!")

Alanna attacked, feeling divorced from her arm as she moved through pass after pass. She saw an opening and her hand took the chance to swing her sword into it. She never took the time to think about what she was doing. Instead, her muscles remembered the patterns of endless drills, repeated over and over with a too-heavy sword. Geoffrey would move to attack or to block, and Alanna's arms and body remembered the move that always followed such an attack or such a block. Sweat poured into Alanna's eyes and she shook it away, stumbling slightly. Geoffrey took advantage of the brief moment of unbalance to lunge in for a strike that would end the bout. Instead Alanna slid Lightning around his sword like a metal snake, twisting her blade deftly. The sword flew from Geoffrey's hand, and he was unable to grab for it. In the same move with which she disarmed him, a panting Alanna presented the tip of her sword at the cloth that covered the bridge of Geoffrey's nose.

The boy stepped back and knelt. "I yield," he said. He looked up at her and grinned. "Well fought, Alan! Very well fought!"

She stared at him, gasping, feeling as if her

lungs were on fire. Then she realized the sound in her ears was cheering. Her friends, in fact all of the pages and squires, were cheering for her.

"Very good, Aram," Duke Gareth murmured to Captain Sklaw. "You've turned out a matchless swordsman."

"'Twasn't me, yer Grace," Sklaw growled, staring at the page who was fumbling at his armor ties. "'Twas the lad Trebond, and he did it all by himself."

～

*T*hat night Jonathan paid a visit to his uncle. "Sir?" he said politely. "I have a favor to ask. It's about this trip to Persopolis in Fief Meron."

The Duke of Naxen grinned. "You know you have only to command me, Jon."

Jonathan chuckled. "But will you obey? Uncle, I'd like Alan to come with us. You said the pages will be going out to Naxen later this summer. He could stay behind then, to make up for it."

The man looked into Jon's face. "This is very unusual, Jonathan."

"I know," was the calm reply. "It's just—Alan spends more time with Gary and Raoul and Alex and me than he does with the pages. I think he'd have more fun if he went with us. And Sir Myles is going, and he's—" The Prince stopped, then went on when he saw an understanding look on his uncle's face. "Myles is a better father to Alan than the Lord of Trebond is. I know we're supposed to speak well of our elders, and Alan never complains, but—we've all got eyes and ears."

The Duke took a nut from a bowl and cracked it. "Does Alan want to go to Persopolis?"

"I don't know," Jonathan said. "Probably, since we're all going. If you mean does he know I'm asking you, no, he doesn't. Knowing Alan, he can't imagine I *would* ask such a favor for him."

"Hm. Have you chosen a squire yet, Jonathan? In case you pass the Ordeal?"

"I'm thinking about one," Jonathan replied calmly. "It isn't an easy decision."

The man thought this over, finally nodding. "As long as the other boys aren't resentful, I don't see why he can't go with you."

Jon smiled. "They won't resent it. Sometimes it seems as if he's just a small squire who takes a lot of interest in what the pages do."

"Very perceptive of you. Will you notify Alan, or do you want me to?"

"You'd better tell him, Uncle. And thank you—from the bottom of my heart." Jonathan kissed the Duke's hand. He was half out the door when the older man's voice stopped him.

"Why does this mean so much to you, Jon?"

The Prince turned. "Because he's my friend. Because I always know where he stands, and where I stand with him. Because I think he'd die for me, and—and I think I'd die for him. Is that enough?"

"You're being pert, nephew," Gareth said with mock sternness. "Have Timon find Alan for me then."

Duke Gareth's news shocked Alanna—she had never expected to be so singled out. She paid careful attention to all his instructions as to her duties during the trip. Since she was to be the only page in the company, she would wait on Lord Martin, Myles and Jonathan and run errands for the troop captain and the squires. She would continue her lessons with Myles as her instructor.

Coram too was pleased with the honor, and his orders to her were as strict as the Duke's. She was to behave. *No pranks* was to be her watchword.

Alanna tried not to let the news go to her head, although she couldn't help but be excited. It surprised her that the other pages were glad for her, rather than jealous. She didn't realize they did not see her as another page—only, as Jonathan had said, as a very small squire.

The night before they rode out, the boys and Myles were summoned to a meeting with Duke Roger. He gathered them in the Great Library, waiting for them to settle down comfortably before speaking. Alanna, tucked down between the large Raoul and the equally large Gary, where she wouldn't attract notice, thought the Duke looked both handsome and impressive, dressed all in sleek black velvet. A strangely designed chain with a sapphire pendant hung around his neck, accenting his eyes.

"Doubtless you lads don't know why I'm talking to you," he said with his easy smile. "I daresay no one's ever mentioned the Black City to you when they've discussed this trip you're taking tomorrow." He shook his dark head. "I don't think it's a good idea to take you all so close, but—well, I was overruled." Alanna was blinking as lights bounced off the sapphire. The shimmering of the jewel was making her sleepy. Angry at herself, she gave her arm a strong pinch. That woke her up. "The Black City is just barely within eye's view of Persopolis," the sorcerer went on. "In fact, the Bazhir have a room specially designed in the western wall of the Persopolis castle. It's called the Sunset Room, and the rumor is the Bazhir had it built so they could always keep an eye on the Black City. As if sheepherders and desert men knew about such things!" He sighed. "You won't be permitted near the City, of course. No one is. It's claimed there's a curse on it, that no mortal being returns from the place alive—especially if he's young. Bazhir stories again, told around the campfires to frighten the children, I've no doubt."

The big man paced the room, a shadow panther with all eyes watching him. "I am certain the Bazhir have created wonderful monsters for their bratlings to fear. That is not why I am cautioning you. There is evil power in the Black City, an immense power that dates far back in time. I do not know its nature. I have never been so foolhardy as to think myself strong enough to fight whatever waits there." Roger had stopped pacing. His eyes were fixed on Jonathan's. "I don't need a seer's crystal to feel the evil in that place from as far away as Persopolis, just as a fisherman doesn't need a special glass to smell a hurricane approaching. If *I* dare not risk it, none of you—untrained, untried—would stand a chance. Don't venture near the Black City, under pain of death and, perhaps, under the pain of losing your souls." He smiled, his eyes locked with Jonathan's. "I know when a sword is too heavy for me to lift."

When Alanna got into bed that night, she was as puzzled as she had ever been. It looked to her as if Roger had dared Jonathan to prove he was more of a man than his cousin, to prove he could brave the Black City that Roger feared. And yet, that couldn't be true. Not even Roger would have the nerve, and the coldness, to send his young cousin to certain death—would he?

seven

~

The Black City

The ride south was the longest and most demanding Alanna had experienced. They were just a day away from Corus when the countryside changed. The hills were rockier. The trees were shrunken and twisted, and the ground plants seemed to fight for each drop of water they took from the earth. The ground itself was brown and dry, torn with cracks. Lizards, snakes and an occasional rabbit looked at the riders as if they were invaders, and the sun felt ten times hotter. By the end of the second day's ride, the cracked earth had turned to sand, and the hills into long dunes. They had reached the Great Southern Desert.

At night Alanna waited on Lord Martin, Myles and the guard captain. She spent several hours of the day riding at Myles's side, learning about the lives and customs of the people of this land. Myles was an interesting teacher, and he knew much about the Southern Desert. Often she caught Lord Martin glancing at the knight with respect in his hard eyes.

Alanna was not the only one taking lessons.

Lord Martin lectured them all on survival in such barren land. Someday their lives might depend on knowing which plants stored water inside or how to find an oasis.

The closer they came to Persopolis, the more Bazhir they encountered. The desert people were hard riders and relentless fighters. They hid their women in goatskin tents. But all, men and women, she sensed, watched the strangers through proud black eyes. Since she had already guessed Lord Martin didn't like his Bazhir subjects, Alanna went to Sir Myles.

"The Bazhir are unusual," the knight admitted. "Martin does have reason to resent them."

"I think he resents everybody," Alanna muttered.

Myles ignored that. "You see, the Old King is said to have conquered all this country as far south as the Inland Sea. Actually, what he conquered was the hill country, to the east, and the coastline from Port Legann to the Tyran River. He never actually conquered this desert—it's far too big. Instead he worked out treaties with some Bazhir and slaughtered a few others. Now some tribes call Roald their king. They trade with the rest of the kingdom and try not to cause any trouble. The others are called renegade. They won't accept Roald as king, and they make life difficult for those who use the Southern Road. The tribe that holds Persopolis is friendly with the King, and that's very important.

Persopolis is the only city built by the Bazhir."

Alanna thought about this for a moment. "Why only one city?" she asked. "And why Persopolis, out in the middle of nowhere?"

"There are five springs in Persopolis," Lord Martin said harshly, bringing his horse up beside them. "As to why only one city—it's said they built it to guard the Black City." He snorted. "Foolishness, if you ask me. Why build a city to guard another that you can scarcely see?" He rode on back down the line.

Alanna squinted at Geoffrey's father. "I don't get it," she said. "He doesn't like the Bazhir—but His Majesty made him overlord of the Desert."

"Martin doesn't like the Bazhir—and they don't like him—but he is fair," Myles replied. "He's fair if it kills him. The Bazhir know that, so they'll deal with him. No one else could have gotten their respect, even if it is grudging." Myles pushed back the hood of the burnoose he had worn since the second day out, looking intently at her. "Why so interested, Alan?"

She shrugged. "No reason—I think. Excuse me. Lord Martin's waving." She wheeled Moonlight and trotted back down the line. She didn't know herself why she was so interested in the desert men.

It took a week to reach Persopolis. At last they could see its granite towers and walls rising before them. The city was built even stronger than fortresses like Trebond, and the weapons carried by its soldiers were well cared for and much used.

People lined the streets to greet their returning lord and to stare at the youth who would one day be their king. While the Bazhir kept to the back of the crowds, watching in silence, the city dwellers waved and called to the young nobles. Jonathan and his friends returned the greetings, as relaxed as if they did this every day, but Alanna guided Moonlight to a spot between Myles and the guard captain and stayed there.

"What's the matter, youngling?" the soldier chuckled. "Shy?"

Alanna blushed. He was right. But there was something else. "Myles?" she asked softly. "Do the Bazhir always stare so?"

The knight tugged his beard thoughtfully. "Actually, they try to ignore us northerners. Perhaps it's Jonathan."

"Um." Alanna's nervous grip on the reins made her horse fidget. She tried to relax. The Bazhir were staring at her, too.

A formal banquet began in the castle late in the afternoon. Everyone wore their finest. There were toasts and long-winded speeches. Myles downed glass after glass of wine, and Alanna hid in a corner unless summoned.

"There you are." Myles was only a little unsteady on his feet. "Are you jealous because Jonathan's the center of attention? He's the prince, lad. He'll be the center of attention for a long time."

He drew a dark, well-dressed man forward. "Here's someone who can tell you more about the Bazhir. Ali Mukhtab, this is Alan of Trebond, our page. Ali Mukhtab is the governor of Persopolis Castle. He is also Bazhir. You two talk—I'm off to a real bed at last." Myles tousled Alanna's hair affectionately and left her alone with Ali Mukhtab.

The page and the man sized each other up carefully. Alanna saw a tall Bazhir with walnut brown skin, glossy black hair and a trimmed black mustache. His large dark eyes were framed with long black lashes, and Alanna was to learn he rarely opened them wide. He did so now, and she shifted uncomfortably. There was power in Mukhtab's gaze. He half closed his eyes once more, smiling sleepily.

"You are not comfortable in this setting," he remarked quietly.

Alanna was never fond of personal remarks. She changed the subject. "I like your vest," she announced. The vest *was* an elegant garment, red velvet trimmed with gold. He smiled, and she knew he had seen through her tactic.

"Sir Myles tells me you are curious about the Bazhir. Why? Surely a young man from a northern fief can have little interest in the desert."

"A person can never tell where he'll end up," she said bluntly. "I understand northerners. I don't understand the Bazhir."

"So. A cat's curiosity, as well as a cat's love of

privacy. Is it permitted to ask why only one page travels in your group?"

Alanna decided she liked this odd man. "His Highness asked if I could come, specially. We're friends—he and I and Gary and Raoul—the two big squires. And Alex—"

"The dark, secretive one," Ali Mukhtab interrupted. "He, too, is like a cat—but not one I would like to know. I am very fond of cats. At least three live in my chambers."

"Alex isn't *secretive,* precisely," Alanna demurred. "He's just—he's always been that way. Can you answer something for me? I know it's a little rude, but I've got to ask."

The Bazhir smiled and accepted two glasses filled with green liquor being passed by a footman. He gave one to Alanna. "Drink," he told her. "You'll like it. By all means, ask me your 'little rude' question."

Alanna sipped the green stuff carefully. It tasted wonderful. "I—uh—I couldn't help but notice that Lord Martin—uh—doesn't much like the Bazhir. I mean, he's supposed to be fair and all—"

Ali Mukhtab grinned outright. "You are right. He is painfully correct with us, and he cannot stand the sight of us. Go on."

"If that's so, why are you a—a Bazhir—the governor of his castle?"

Mukhtab turned his glass in his fingers. "Your friend Myles said you were intelligent. He did not say you were blunt."

Alanna blushed. "Myles said that about *me?*" Her blush deepened. "I never said I was tactful," she added.

"The post of governor in the castle of Persopolis goes by right to a Bazhir," Ali Mukhtab explained. "Lord Martin cannot change that, although I know he has tried to. It is in the treaty with the Old King. I think our people would rise up if the king in the north tried to change the custom."

"Over one castle position?" Alanna asked. "That seems a little—well, extreme."

"There is a very good reason for that tradition," the Bazhir explained. He looked out the window at the dimming sky. "In fact, if you and your friends can leave discreetly, I will show you all something interesting."

ᔐ

Within a few minutes Alanna and her friends had assembled in a back hallway. Jonathan was the last to arrive; he had more difficulty sneaking away.

"If I hear one more noble tell me he'd like to see a green city once again before he dies—" the Prince muttered, his patience obviously worn thin. "What's up?"

Alanna performed hasty introductions, and the young men followed the governor down the hallway.

"I must admit to surprise," Ali Mukhtab was saying to Jonathan. "I did not think Alan's message would lure you away from those who were so anxious to have you like them."

"You took the sword by the point," Jonathan replied, tweaking Alanna's nose. "If I were anyone else, they wouldn't have two words to say to me. But I'm the prince, and I think every man in that room wanted something from me—except Lord Martin," he added, nodding to Geoffrey. "I didn't come here to have people treating me as if I'm made of gold."

They stopped before a wooden door. Mukhtab produced a brass key that matched the lock and handle. "This is the Sunset Room," he told them, unlocking the door. "Only the governor of the castle holds the key."

The five boys looked at each other. This was the room Duke Roger had mentioned, the room built to watch the Black City. Its design was totally different from that of any other room in the castle. The stone floors and walls had been coated with small, brightly colored tiles, which formed pictures. Many were of the Black City and of the Bazhir. Alanna peered closely at the walls, touching them with gentle fingers.

"It's very old," she said finally.

"Even we do not know how old it is," Ali Mukhtab replied. The door opened once again. Servants appeared with pillows and refreshments. The boys wandered over to the wall that looked out to the west. There was no window to block out the desert air. Only the posts supporting the ceiling separated the Sunset Room from the view.

The room was set high in the Persopolis wall. Before them stretched the Great Southern Desert, as far as their eyes could see. It was a magnificent sight, painted red-gold by the setting sun. The view's only flaw was that it faced the west, and the dying light shone directly into their eyes.

Suddenly Jonathan pointed. "That small black speck—just where the sun is. That's the Black City?"

Ali Mukhtab nodded. "That is the Black City, the doom of my people for centuries. Ever since we can remember—and our memories reach beyond the days when your palace, Highness, was a palace for the Old Ones—our young people have been called to the Black City. Our masters lived there, the Nameless Ones. They stole our souls and gave us farms and cattle. We swore never to farm again. Legends say we stopped there when we came north, over the Inland Sea. The Nameless Ones welcomed us and asked us to share their land and farm their crops. All this, the legends say, was green and fertile." Ali's hand swept over the leagues of empty sand. "When we saw that they were stealing our spirits, we rebelled. We burned them and their city, and all the land turned to dust. After we left, never to return, we built Persopolis, so that we might watch the City, always."

"How could you burn them out, if they were so

powerful?" Gary wanted to know.

"They feared fire above all things," the man replied. "Their spirits linger in the City, but they cannot pass the circle of fire we placed around their walls."

"You said they call your young people," Alex said. "What do you mean?"

The man sighed. "Sometimes a youth or a maiden will awaken in the night and try to ride to the City. If they are stopped, they rave and scream and refuse their food, talking only of the City and of the gods who wish them to come there. If we do not let them go, they starve themselves to death."

"And if they go, they don't come back," Jonathan said quietly.

"Isn't it better to let them go?" Raoul asked. "Maybe it isn't the City at all. Your life is—well, it's harsh. Maybe they really go on to other cities, to live somewhere else."

"We would like to think so," the governor of the castle replied. "But we have trained our young to be honest." His eyes were on Alanna as he said this, and she squirmed. "Those who leave us for the cities go with their families' blessings—or curses—but they always tell us that is where they go. Those who want the Black City speak only of it, as if they could not lie about it if they tried."

"It seems cruel to me to tie them up and keep them." Raoul yawned, settling onto a pillow and pouring himself a glass of wine.

"To the Bazhir, even death by starvation is better than the fate we think awaits them there," Ali Mukhtab said. "We have another legend—the Bazhir have many legends—that says one day we will be free of the call of the City. It says two gods, the Night One and the Burning-Brightly One, will go into the City to battle with the immortals there. I do not know how true that may be." The Bazhir smiled. "Some, like Lord Martin, say we have many legends because we possess little else. He is probably right."

"Your people seem to be old and wise," Jonathan said. He was standing by the window, watching the last pool of sun disappear into the desert. "It's too bad no one has written a history of the Bazhir."

Ali Mukhtab looked at him. His eyes opened wide, fixing Jonathan with his strangely intent gaze. "Are you interested in such things, Highness?"

Jonathan returned that powerful look evenly. "I have to be," he said. "The Bazhir will be my people too, someday."

Mukhtab bowed low. "I will see if such a history can be found—or written."

"I look forward to reading it," the Prince replied. He followed his friends out into the hall.

"What a story." Raoul grinned. "Ghouls and ghosts—I wonder what the truth was?"

"The mosaics on the walls hinted that the truth was pretty frightening," Alex told him.

"The mosaics were done by the Bazhir," Gary pointed out. "Come on. It's bedtime and past."

They made their way to their rooms, not noticing that Alan and Jon lingered behind.

"I wonder who they *really* were," Alanna mused. "The Nameless Ones."

Jon's voice was casual. "An old enemy, made bigger to scare the young ones, I guess. It's a sensible idea. There are probably a lot of places in those ruins where a child could get lost. Good night, Alan."

She glanced sharply at him. First he was very interested in the Bazhir, and now he was saying their legends were stories to scare children. That wasn't like Jonathan. The carefully innocent look on his face wasn't like Jonathan, either.

"Good night," she murmured, turning into her chamber. No one was waiting up for her, Coram being back at the palace. If anyone had thought Alan might get into more trouble than usual without his eagle-eyed servant to watch him, no one had mentioned it.

Alanna blew out the lamp and undressed in the dark, still wondering about Jonathan's turnabout behavior.

✑

She wakened suddenly, before dawn. Every nerve in her body quivered, as if she were about to take a test in the practice yards. She dressed swiftly, binding herself tight and pulling a loose blue shirt over her head. She tucked the shirt into her breeches, then struggled to get her riding boots over her stockinged feet. Hands trembling, she buckled Lightning and her dagger at her side. She didn't know why she was in such a hurry, and she didn't stop to think about it, either. At last she was ready and slid out into the hall.

A light burned in Jonathan's room. Suddenly it went out. His door opened. Alanna, tucked into a dark niche, watched as the Prince slipped into the hall, fully dressed.

"You must be crazy," she hissed as he closed his door.

His eyes searched until he found her in the shadows. His teeth flashed in a grin. "Are you coming? I'm going, with you or without you."

She followed, her well-used boots padding like cat feet on the floor. No one was awake down at the stables. Quickly they saddled their horses. A gold coin bought the cooperation of the large Bazhir stationed at the city gate. Together they rode swiftly into the west.

∾

*T*here was no sand in the Black City, no dust—nothing to show that centuries had passed since people lived there. The streets were hard, black and bare, shining in the sun. The alien buildings—beautifully and carefully carved—rose without break from the rock of the streets. If any tower was not part of the mass of rock beneath their feet, they did not find it. The city rose like a cluster of needles stabbing into the sky.

"It's very nice," Alanna said with approval when they were just inside the gate. "Now let's go back." She remembered suddenly the vision she had seen of a black city, not once but twice. Was she meant to be here? Well, if she was, she was scared.

"You can go," her friend replied, running a hand over a carving. "I'm looking around some more."

Alanna shrugged and followed, her hand on Lightning's hilt. Maybe this was what she had to do. They explored silently, peering into echoing buildings while the noon sun beat down on their heads. The great towers were bare of everything—furniture, cloth, glass—except the carving that covered the entire city.

Alanna examined these carvings with care. They showed strange animals and stranger people: men with the heads of lions, women with bird's wings, great cats with human faces. Alanna had never seen anything like it. Now that she had, she wished she hadn't.

"I don't see bodies or skeletons," Jonathan whispered. "Those young Bazhir probably just took off for the cities."

"Then why are you whispering?" Her voice was equally soft.

The Prince looked around, searching the windows and doorways. "I'm not sure— Yes, I am. This place is evil. Whatever has or hasn't happened here, the city is still evil, through and through."

"I'm glad we left the horses outside," was her only answer. As they ventured deeper and deeper into the city, she kept close watch on the doors and windows around them.

They turned a sharp corner, and the city's central square lay before them. It was a wide, flat reach of stone, carefully polished and yet reflecting no light from its surface. Alanna decided it was like staring into a huge pit covered with glass. It took all her nerve to step onto it, but step she did. The building in the center of the square called to her. Its sides were columns of plain black stone. The roof separated itself from the columns with a border of carving covered with gold. Topping a long rise of stairs, great doors beckoned. She and Jonathan climbed up to the doors, feeling smaller and smaller as they climbed. The doors stood open and waiting. Like the stone of the city, the black wood of the doors was covered with exotic pictures. The edges of the carvings were lined with gold.

When they reached the doors, Lightning began humming, its hilt trembling in Alanna's hand. "Jonathan—my sword—" she stammered.

"Hm?" The Prince was eyeing the doors.

"I don't think we should go in. My sword is—it's *humming*."

Jonathan shook his head. "I'm going to find out what's going on." He stepped inside the temple.

Alanna tightened her grip on her sword hilt and followed. "You know I can't let you come in here by yourself," she snapped as she caught up with him.

Jonathan grinned at her. "Of course. Why did you think I asked Uncle to let you come?"

"You planned this all along!" she accused.

"I hate mysteries. This place has been one for years. I knew you'd have the guts to come with me."

"But—Gary, Alex, Raoul," she protested. "They would've—"

"They would've grumbled all the way here and then knocked me over the head when I tried to enter the city. I knew you'd come and keep quiet."

"That's because I'm the only one with insanity in my family," she grumbled.

Jonathan laughed, and the sound was eaten up by the air inside the temple. They walked forward slowly, their hands on their sword hilts. There were no windows or torches, but a weird yellow-green light came from somewhere. The walls were carved from the glassy stone, catching the light and making it ripple along their surfaces. At the end of the chamber was a large block of dark stuff that swallowed the light without reflecting it.

"The altar," Jonathan whispered.

The light moved in a blinding wave across the room. When the eyes of the two humans cleared, ten men and women were standing in front of the altar. Even the smallest of the women was taller than Duke Gareth, and they were all so beautiful that it hurt to look at them for very long. Their power flashed and rippled around their bodies in a dance of green light.

"It has been so long," a woman in red said with a sigh." "And they are so small."

One woman stretched a hand out to them. Her fingernails were long and red, like claws. "Feel the life in them, Ylira. It is a flame. These two will be enough for us all."

Alanna edged closer to Jonathan's side. Lightning was trembling in her grip. "This was *your* idea," she muttered.

"Who are you?" Jonathan demanded of the strangers. His voice was clear and calm. He showed no sign of fear.

"They speak," a man-being sneered. "And look at the little one. It will hit us with its sword."

The beings—the Nameless Ones—laughed. Alanna shivered at the cruelty in the sound.

The largest of the men waved a careless hand. He was broad-shouldered and black-bearded, a giant even among these creatures. "Your mortal weapons will not hurt us," he boomed. "We are the Ysandir. We are immortal. Our flesh is not like yours."

"You cannot keep us here," Jonathan replied steadily.

"We are hungry." The clawed woman's eyes glinted. "We have not fed for one of your years. The goatherders are too good at keeping their young from us."

A woman with hair whiter than snow purred, "He thinks his father the king will hunt for them and destroy us."

They laughed. Alanna wanted to put her hands over her ears and shut out that dreadful sound. But she forced herself to remain still, moving her feet so she would be totally balanced when the attack came.

The black-bearded one smiled. "I am Ylon, chief of the Ysandir. I have fed on hundreds of your mortal lives. Let your father bring his armies. We will feed on their souls, and we will be strong. We will break the curse of fire the Bazhir put on this place."

Jonathan took a deep breath. "I don't need my father's soldiers. I am going to leave here, and you are not going to keep me."

"Listen to the princeling!" mocked the red-clawed woman. "How you roar, young lion!"

"Don't you *dare* speak so to him!" Alanna cried. She drew Lightning in a swift movement. The crystal on the hilt blazed out, throwing a harsh light into the darkness around them. The Ysandir shrank back against the altar, trying to keep the light from their eyes.

"So. You come armed with *their* weapons," Ylon said. "But can you use them?"

"Ylanda," said Ylira, the woman in red. "I cannot see into this one's mind. It is hiding something. Where did you get the sword?" she snapped, staring at Alanna.

"None of your business!" Alanna replied, focusing on the red-gowned being. For a second she felt a touch in her mind, like claws raking through her head. She yelled. Lightning flashed, and the woman with claws—Ylanda—collapsed against the altar. She was gasping for breath.

"Don't give them an opening like that again," Jonathan warned. Already the air around him was shimmering with blue light. Alanna brought up her own shield of violet magic, keeping Lightning outside—just in case.

"I didn't plan to give them that one," she murmured.

Ylanda had gotten her breath back. Suddenly she was laughing. The others watched her. "In all my centuries," she gasped finally, "I have not known such a jest. Young lion—see your companion for what she really is!"

"She?" Jonathan whispered.

Before Alanna could bring Lightning's crystal up, power from Ylanda and Ylon smashed into her defenses, breaking through. She doubled over in pain. It was over as swiftly as it began, with one difference. Her clothes were gone. All she wore was her belt and scabbard.

The Ysandir were laughing with Ylanda. "A girl! His boy companion was a girl!"

The one called Ylira laughed scornfully as Alanna tried to cover herself with her hands. "A girl who hopes to protect her prince? A jest indeed!"

Alanna held up Lightning's crystal, letting its light burn into their eyes. The crystal dimmed, and she shouted, "I may be a girl, but I can defend—or attack!—as well as any boy!" She looked at Jonathan. Her friend was openly staring. "Highness," she whispered, blushing a deep red. "I—"

He pulled off his tunic and handed it to her. "Later. Just—who are you?"

She pulled the tunic on. Jon was so tall that his tunic covered her thighs—a small thing, but one she appreciated just now. "Alanna of Trebond, Highness."

Ylon's booming voice pulled their attention back to their enemies. "Separate them."

Instinctively Alanna gripped Jonathan's hand. Sapphire and amethyst power collected at their intertwined fingers.

"The Wall of Power," Jonathan hissed. "What's the spell?"

Alanna started the verses. Jon's voice joined hers, the words thundering in the great chamber. Slowly a wall of blue-violet light rose between them and the Ysandir. The immortals covered their eyes, unable to look at it for long. They retreated.

"You defy us?" Ylon cried. "Pay the price, mortals!

Tearing pain shot through their joined hands.

"Don't let them part us," Jon said. He held on so tightly Alanna's bones creaked. She ignored the pain, keeping her mind on the Wall. The Ysandir came closer, their bodies shining with yellow-green magic. Furious, they threw bolts of power at their prey. Jon and Alanna concentrated, bringing up all their will power to keep their defenses strong. The Wall stood. Two immortals touched it and screamed. They vanished with a flash.

"So you *can* die," Alanna taunted. "You *can* feel pain."

"How long do you think she will last?" Ylira asked Jonathan, softly. "Another few moments? Not even that? She is a girl. She is weak. She will give way, and where will you be?"

It was the same small voice that taunted Alanna from within whenever she faced a taller, stronger opponent.

"You think so?" she shouted furiously. "Then try *this* on for size!"

A slender thread of violet fire snaked through the wall, wrapping itself around Ylira's throat and tightening. The immortal did not even have the chance to scream before she fell to the ground and vanished.

Alanna didn't have time to gloat. Three women joined hands to form a deadly-looking triangle. Power collected at the center of their formation in a small, evil ball.

"Jonathan?" Alanna whispered. This kind of magic was beyond her, but she knew Jonathan had spent more time studying books of sorcery than she had.

Jonathan spoke, using words she had never heard before. Alanna felt her own magic flowing into her friend's body. Slowly the Prince reached through the Wall. Magic lanced from his fingertips, shattering the triangle. Alanna blinked, trying to clear her eyes of the blaze that had been the three Ysandir.

Five remained. The redheaded woman and the brunette with the hungry eyes screamed and threw themselves on the Wall. They blazed and vanished. The others drew back.

Alanna remembered something. "Jon—fire?" she hissed.

"Of course," he whispered.

Duke Roger had not taught them that spell, but Duke Gareth had. The pages had been camping in the royal forests. Before that night most of them had not known Duke Gareth possessed the Gift.

"It's the first spell any Naxen learns, if he has the Gift," the Duke explained. "Put that flint away, Alex—I'll show you."

Together now Alanna and Jonathan whispered the spell Duke Gareth taught them, changing some words to meet their need.

> "Bright flame, light fire—
> Around Ysandir burn higher.
> Light the fire, bright the flame—
> Burn Ysandir in Mithros' name."

"Ylon!" cried one of the two male Ysandir remaining. Fire roared up outside the Wall, reaching with eager fingers for the one who cried out. He screamed and disappeared, the fire vanishing with him.

Only two remained of the Ysandir: Ylon and Ylanda. Alanna gulped. These two had joined hands, and power gathered to them.

"*Ak-hoft!*" Ylon cried. The Wall vanished as if it had never been.

"The others were weak and greedy," Ylon said with a sneer. "We are not."

"We are the First," Ylanda added. "We were here before all the others. We shall remain."

"Who are you?" Jonathan asked, trying to catch his breath. Alanna wiped her sweat-beaded face on her sleeve. She was tired, so tired her bones ached.

"We are gods and the children of gods," the woman said. "We were here before your Old Ones, and we laughed when their cities fell."

Alanna felt a return of her old spirit. "A likely story," she said with a sniff. "Gods don't die. You do."

"You think you know all, mortal. You know nothing. Even immortals die when they weaken. Ylanda and I are the strongest. You will not weaken us."

"You give a lot of big talk," Alanna retorted. "I believe in deeds, not words."

Jonathan's voice was even and strong. "Your time is past. You no longer belong here."

Ylon and Ylanda raised their linked hands, chanting in a language that made the two humans shudder. Outside thunder crashed. The weird glow that lighted the temple vanished. The only light now came from their magics.

"Jonathan?" Alanna whispered.

He looked down at her. "We're not beaten yet. Alanna—can you become what you were the night you saved me from the fever? When you brought me back from death?"

"I don't know," she whispered, eyeing the Ysandir.

"You have to—and you must take me with you. Otherwise—"

Jonathan didn't have to elaborate. The light of the immortals' magic was getting stronger.

Alanna looked at their linked hands, shining with the blue-violet of their combined Gifts. Already she was falling out of herself into that light. She could feel Jonathan with her. Her eyes burned as their magic grew brighter and formed a globe around them.

"Goddess," she whispered in her woman's voice. "Great Mother—"

"Dark Lady," a man added softly, "open the Way for us." Did she really hear Jonathan the man? She wasn't sure.

Needle-sharp bolts of magic were lancing into their interlocked hands. Pain shot through their physical shells. Ylon and Ylanda stood before them in a wheel of yellow-green power. Fire streamed from them and broke on the newly formed globe of magic that held the bodies of Jon and Alanna.

For the second time in her life Alanna heard that female voice, the one that made her scream with pain. This time she didn't scream. She was too busy concentrating on keeping their globe of power in one piece.

The voice echoed in her mind. *Place your trust in the sword—and fight.*

Alanna had dropped Lightning during the earlier fight. Now the sword jumped into her free hand, the crystal blazing. She could feel it trembling as she gripped the hilt.

"Just don't let go of me," Jonathan cautioned.

"I won't." Holding Jonathan fast, she stepped forward. Lightning sang in her hand.

A black, two-edged blade appeared in Ylon's free hand. Like Jonathan, Ylanda did not let go of her companion. She stayed close, keeping step behind him.

Ylon brought his sword down in a ferocious arc. Alanna blocked it swiftly, her arm muscles screaming as she stopped the down-sweeping blade. Lightning blazed and—miraculously—did not break. The dark sword drank in Lightning's fire as Ylon backed away. His big chest was heaving, and there was sweat on his face. Alanna circled him, her eyes never leaving his sword. Jonathan squeezed her hand reassuringly.

She felt better now. *This* was what she had trained for. She turned all her attention to the swords, letting Jonathan control their sorcery. Ylon, suddenly wary of her, lanced at her in a series of rapid thrusts. Alanna stopped each of them, feeling her confidence grow each time she stopped the Ysandir. Immortal he might be—swordsman he was not.

Jonathan was speaking softly, uttering words she paid no attention to. The fire surrounding him and Alanna blazed, and the girl yelled with triumph. She swung Lightning up and around in a complex move that brought the swords together, hilt to hilt. Ylon's sword shattered with the impact. Alanna slashed at the immortals' linked hands. The globe of yellow-green light exploded, and the two Ysandir screamed with rage and fear. Jonathan uttered one word of command, throwing the last reserves of their Gift into the spell. Blue-violet light flooded over the immortals. They flared up like a giant torch as everything went black.

∾

*A*lanna and Jonathan awoke on the floor of the chamber. The Ysandir had vanished. Only a scorch mark in the perfect floor remained of Ylon and Ylanda. Near Alanna was Lightning, the sword's tip blackened.

"Are you all right?" Jonathan asked wearily. He pulled himself to his feet.

Alanna couldn't swallow a tiny moan. Every muscle screamed with pain. "I'm smarting a little," she admitted. "How about you?"

"'Smarting' is an understatement. Come on. I want to get away from here before we try to rest." Jonathan stumbled over to her sword and picked it up. "It's still warm," he said with awe.

Alanna rose, somehow. She felt as if someone had pounded her with hammers. "Think there are any more of them?" She accepted her sword and sheathed it carefully.

The Prince shook his head. "I'd say we've seen the last of the Ysandir. Come. We'll lean on each other."

They made it somehow to the city walls, where Moonlight and Darkness waited patiently for them. Jonathan felt his saddle, then the saddle blanket. "They're wet," he said. "It's been raining out here."

Alanna pulled herself onto her mare's back with her last bit of strength. She had no wish to comment.

Jonathan headed east, to a small oasis they knew was nearer the Black City than Persopolis. Alanna wasn't about to argue that they were going the wrong way. The oasis was closer than home, and all she wanted to do was lie down.

The horses contentedly cropped grass while their owners bathed their aching faces and hands in the cool water. Jonathan finally leaned back against a palm tree. "I wish I'd thought to bring food."

Alanna lay flat on the grass nearby. "I'm happy just to be alive."

They rested in silence for a while, breathing the fresh desert air deeply. They watched the sun set in pools of rose and orange, thinking they had never seen a lovelier sunset. Darkness came, and thousands of stars.

"Moonrise soon," Alanna said at last. "We could try for Persopolis then."

"We'd never make it." Jonathan's quiet voice came from the shadows. "We're in trouble as it is. Spending the night won't make it any worse."

There was a long silence once again. Finally Alanna said, "I suppose you'd like an explanation."

"Yes."

She sighed. "It's a long story."

"We have time," he said comfortably. "I don't intend to move till I hear it. You must admit, I've had a shock."

"I'm sorry," she said humbly. "I haven't wanted to lie to you."

"I should hope so. You're the worst liar I've ever met." He thought about this a moment, then added, "—or the best. Now I'm all confused. What about your twin?"

"He didn't want to be a knight," she replied simply. "He wants to be a great sorcerer." She sighed. "Today was more Thom's sort of thing than mine. Father was going to send me to the convent and Thom to the palace. And I didn't want to learn to be a lady." Jonathan's chuckle gave her courage. "Old Maude knew. She said it was right. And—well, I talked Coram around."

Jonathan knew Coram well. "How?" he asked curiously.

"I threatened to make him see things that were not there. He doesn't like that."

Jon chuckled again, imagining Coram seeing visions. "And your father?"

"He doesn't care about Thom or me," she said flatly. "I want to be a warrior maiden and do great deeds. Thom likes sorcery, and Father hates it. The only way we could get what we wanted—was to lie. I had to pretend to be a boy. I was always better at the fighting arts than Thom anyway."

"Whose idea was it to make the switch?"

"Mine," she admitted ruefully. "Thom might have thought of it, but he's the careful one. I knew what I wanted, and I didn't mind taking a risk or two." She sighed. "I enjoyed the life."

"You could've been caught at any time. You could've been a weakling; Roger could've found out."

"There've been warrior maids before. They weren't weak. And—well, I think my Gift protects me from Duke Roger. I'm not sure, but I think so. And you can't say I haven't proved myself."

"Of course you have, often. You do better than most of us."

She picked at the grass. "I had to."

"Alanna. It's a pretty name," he said thoughtfully. "Thom. Maude. Coram. Who else knows?"

"George, and his mother."

"*You* trusted *George?*"

"He can be trusted!" she said hotly. "Besides—I needed help once, and I knew he'd never give me away. He's my friend, Jon."

"You called me 'Jon.'"

"You saved my life, back there."

"You saved mine. We wouldn't have made it without each other. I knew I was right to take you."

She lay silent for a while, listening to the sounds in the night. At last she gathered her courage. "What're you going to do about me?"

His voice was surprised. "Do? I'm not doing anything. As far as I'm concerned, you earned the right to try for your shield a long time ago." She heard him moving. "No one will learn your secret from me, Alanna."

Her chin trembled. Tears stung her eyes. "Thank you, your Highness."

He knelt beside her. "I thought you were calling me Jon. Alanna, you're crying."

"It's been such an awful day," she sobbed. Hesitantly the young man put his arms around her and drew her against him. "And now you're being so kind." She wept into his shirt.

"Not kind," he told her. "Grateful. Admiring. You're getting my shirt wet."

She laughed and straightened, wiping her eyes.

"I'm sorry, Jon. I haven't done that for a long time."

"I believe it," he said, sitting back on his heels. "I don't think you cried even when Ralon was beating on you, and you were just a little boy—girl. Mithros, I'm confused!" he whistled. "Gods, that's why you never went swimming! All the times you've seen us naked—*me* naked!"

She gripped his arm. "Jon, you start to act like that, and I'm finished. You've got to go on treating me like any other boy, or I'm through!"

He sat beside her. "What insanity! But you're right." She could feel his eyes on her face although it was too dark to see him clearly. "How do you plan to be a warrior maiden if no one knows you're a girl?"

"I'm going to tell everyone, on my eighteenth birthday."

"What will you do after that?" She could see him grin. "Mithros, Uncle will have fits."

She relaxed. "I'm going to travel and do great deeds."

He ruffled her hair. "I believe you. Don't forget your friends when you're a legend."

She laughed. "You'll be more famous than me! You'll be king one day!"

"And I'll need all my friends. Will you still serve me when you're doing great deeds?"

"I'm your vassal," she said seriously. "I'll never forget that."

"Excellent." He rose with a slight moan. "I want

to keep one of the best fencers at Court on my side. I'm going to bathe. Don't watch."

She grinned. "I never watch." She turned her back as he walked down to the water. Dreamily she stared at the sky, listening to Jon yelp as he splashed chilly water over his aching body.

His voice startled her when he spoke. "You're only that quiet when you're worrying about something. What's bothering you now?"

"Two things," she admitted. "The Ysandir—we have no way of knowing they're gone for good or that we got all of them."

"*I* know that we did," Jonathan replied. "Sometimes a man has to rely on his instincts. The Ysandir are gone forever."

"Doesn't it seem—well, strange—that a boy and a girl were able to destroy the Bazhir demons?"

"You're forgetting," he reminded her gently, "we had help. Even the Bazhir demons couldn't stand against the gods."

"I suppose so," she said dubiously.

"I *know* so." Jonathan climbed from the pool and hurried into his clothes. "Your turn. And keep talking—it'll frighten any animals away."

"Don't you watch," she warned as she stripped and plunged into the chilly water.

Jonathan chuckled. "Not me. You're too skinny—and too good with a sword. You said two things were bothering you. What's the other one?"

Alanna shook soggy hair from her eyes, trying

to decide how she could best say what she was thinking. She was about to tread on very dangerous ground. "Doesn't it strike you as odd—the way Duke Roger warned us to stay away from the Black City?" She climbed out of the oasis and pulled on the over-large tunic once more.

"You mean the way he practically dared us— well, me—to come here."

Alanna sat beside him, trying to see her friend's face in the desert night. "You *knew?*" she whispered, horrified. "You knew Duke Roger was sending you to almost certain death?"

His grip on her arm was painful. "Now *that* I do not believe," he said sternly. "Roger is my only cousin and one of my best friends. He taught me to ride! He would never—*never*—do the thing you're suggesting, Alanna. Never. He sent me here because he thought I might have a chance to rid Tortall of a scourge, and I did, with your help. He must have known I'd take you with me; I'm sure by now he has the whole story of what happened the night I had the Sweating Fever. He did Tortall a favor, and he did me a favor. People will think twice before they take on a prince—or a king—who can defeat demons."

"Why didn't he do it himself?" she asked. "Why risk the only heir to the throne?"

"Perhaps he doesn't have the—the other powers helping him, as they seem to be helping us. And that's enough for this discussion. I would trust

Roger with my life, and with yours. If he had ever wanted the throne, he could have had it any time all these years past. So let's change the subject, all right?"

There are too many perhaps in all that, Alanna thought rebelliously, but she did as she was told. After all, Jon was older, wiser and far better acquainted with Duke Roger. But she still thought the Duke of Conté never expected them to return from the Black City.

They both found comfortable spots beneath the same tree, stretching out for a night's sleep. Alanna was gazing at the distant outline of the Black City when Jon said, "Alan. Alanna. Perhaps you'll help me with a decision I have to make."

Relief made her smile. At least he wasn't angry because she had said what she had about his cousin. "I can try."

"What with Gary and Alex and Raoul becoming knights at the same time I do, it makes competition for the squires pretty fierce."

"So I've noticed," she said dryly.

He chuckled. "Who do you think I should pick?"

Alanna sat up on her elbow. A week ago she would have told him to pick Geoffrey or Douglass. But she had not been to the Black City then. She had not proved to the Ysandir that a girl could be one of the worst enemies they would ever face.

But what if she had not gone to the Black City?

Duke Gareth had mentioned that, with a deal more practice, she could become one of the finest swordsmen at Court. In archery she hit the target every time. The masters who taught her tactics and logic said she was sometimes brilliant—Myles said she was far more intelligent than many adults. She had bested Ralon of Malven, and in some strange way she had won her sword.

All at once she felt different inside her own skin.

"Me," she said at last. "You should pick me."

"But you're a girl." It was impossible to tell what he was thinking.

"So?" she demanded. "Even Captain Sklaw says I'll be a swordsman yet. I'm as good an archer as Alex, and he's a boy and a squire. I'm a better tracker than Raoul. And have I ever failed you? Back there, or when you had the Fever—"

"I'm glad you agree with my reasons," he interrupted calmly. "I told Father you'd probably accept."

Alanna swallowed hard.

"Before we left, I told him I wanted you for my squire. He didn't seem very surprised." Jonathan wriggled, trying to find a softer spot on the ground.

"B-but," Alanna stuttered, "isn't it different? Now that you know—"

"That you're a girl? No, not in the way you mean. Girl, boy or dancing bear, you're the finest page—the finest squire-to-be—at Court." He chuckled. "I almost had to fight Gary for you. He said it wasn't fair, me getting the best because I'm the prince." He took her hand. "Alanna of Trebond—I will be honored if you will serve as my squire."

Alanna kissed his hand, blinking back tears. "My life and sword are yours, Highness."

He spoiled the dignity of the moment by ruffling her hair. "Now, get some sleep." He settled back and closed his eyes. "You know," he murmured, "I'd almost rather face old Ylon again than Lord Martin in a temper."

"I'll blame it all on you," she replied sleepily. "See if I don't."

He dozed off quickly. Alanna lay awake a little while longer, watching the dark towers of the Black City in the distance. If there were any more Ysandir about, she was too tired to care. She wished she had Jon's faith in Duke Roger, but knew she wasn't going to get it. Still, she could figure out the Duke of Conté later. As Jon said, there was morning and Lord Martin to face, and it was time at last to sleep.

～

The Beginning

*T*AMORA PIERCE was born in western Pennsylvania in 1954, has lived in various states across America, and currently resides in Manhattan. A graduate of the University of Pennsylvania, she studied social work, film, and psychology. She has been a martial arts movie reviewer, housemother in a group home, a literary agent's assistant, head writer for a radio production company, and an investment banking secretary. She is married to writer/filmmaker Tim Liebe. They are owned by two cats (the Lioness, better known as Scrap, and Vinnie) and by Zorak, an attitudinal parakeet.

Ms. Pierce began writing stories when she was eleven. Her published books include the Song of the Lioness quartet (*Alanna: The First Adventure, In the Hand of the Goddess, The Woman Who Rides Like a Man,* and *Lioness Rampant*) and the Immortals quartet (*Wild Magic, Wolf-Speaker, Emperor Mage,* and *The Realms of the Gods*), which have also been translated into German and Danish. Ms. Pierce has already started working on her next series.

~

Alanna's adventures have only started...

Here's a preview of the next
Song of the Lioness book

In the Hand of the Goddess

now a Random House Fantasy paperback.

The copper-haired rider looked at the black sky and swore. The storm would be on her soon, and she was hours away from shelter. No matter what she did, she was going to have to spend the night out-of-doors.

"I *hate* getting wet," Alanna of Trebond told her mare. "I don't like being cold, either, and we'll probably be both."

The horse whickered in reply, flicking her white tail. Alanna sighed and patted Moonlight's neck— she also didn't like exposing her faithful mare to such conditions.

They were on the last leg of an errand in the coastal hills. A forest lay before them; beyond it was the Great Road South and a half a day's ride to the capital city and home. Alanna shook her head. They could probably find shelter somewhere under the trees, if luck was with them.

Clucking to Moonlight, she picked up their pace. In the distance thunder rolled, and a few drops of rain blew into her face. She shivered and swore again. Checking to make sure the scroll she carried was safe in its waterproof wrapping and tucked between her tunic and shirt, Alanna shrugged into a hooded cloak. Her friend Myles of Olau would be very upset if the three-hundred-year-old document she had been sent to fetch got wet!

Moonlight carried her under the trees, where Alanna peered through the growing darkness. If they rode too much longer, it would be impossible to find dry firewood even in a forest this thick. The rain was falling now in fat drops. It would be nice if she could find an abandoned hut, or even an occupied one, but she knew better than to expect that.

Something hit the back of her gloved hand with a wet smack—a huge, hairy wood-spider. Alanna yelled and threw the thing off her, startling Moonlight. The gold mare pranced nervously until her mistress got her under control once more. For a moment Alanna sat and shook, huddled into her cloak.

I hate spiders, she thought passionately. *I just— loathe spiders.* She shook her head in disgust and gathered the reins in still-trembling hands. Her fellow squires at the palace would laugh if they knew she feared spiders. They'd say she was behaving like a girl, not knowing she *was* a girl.

"What do they know about girls anyway?" she asked Moonlight as they moved on. "Maids at the palace handle snakes and kill spiders without acting silly. Why do boys say someone acts like a girl as if it were an insult?"

Alanna shook her head, smiling a little. In the three years she had been disguised as a boy, she had learned that boys know girls as little as girls know boys. It didn't make sense—*people are people, after all,* she thought—but that was how things were.

A hill rose sharply to the left of the road. Crowning it was an old willow tree thick with branches. It would take hours for the rain to soak through onto the ground under that tree, if it soaked through at all, and there was room between the limbs and trunk for both Alanna and Moonlight.

Within moments she had Moonlight unsaddled and covered with a blanket. The mare fed on grass under the tree as Alanna gathered dry sticks, branches and leaves. With some struggle and much swearing—her first teacher in woodcraft, Coram, was a soldier, and she had learned plenty of colorful language from him—she got a fire going. When it was burning well, she gathered large branches that were a little wet, putting them beside the fire to dry. Coram had taught her all this when she was a child at Trebond, planning to be a warrior maiden when she grew up.

There was only one problem with her ambition, Coram had explained when she told him what she wanted to be. The last warrior maiden had died a hundred years ago. Nobly born girls went to convent schools and became ladies. Boys became warriors, particularly their fathers' heirs, like Alanna's twin brother Thom, who was often reading, generally books about sorcery. Thom was no warrior, just as Alanna—who had the Gift of magic as well as he did—was no sorceress. She hated and feared her magic; Thom wanted to be the greatest sorcerer living.

Alanna frowned and took food from her saddlebags. She didn't want to think about Thom now, when she was tired and a little lonely.

She sneezed twice and looked up, sharply scanning the clearing beyond the screen of willow branches. When supernatural things were about to happen her nose itched; she didn't know why. And now the *feel* of the clearing had changed. Quickly she shoved the cloak back, freeing her arms. Searching the darkness with wide violet eyes, Alanna loosened her sword, Lightning.

Moonlight whickered, backing against the willow. "Something wrong, girl?" Alanna asked. She sneezed again and rubbed her nose.

A sound came from the trees behind her. She spun, unsheathing Lightning in the same movement. The sound was repeated, and Alanna frowned. If she didn't know better , she would swear something had *mewed* out there! Then she laughed, sliding Lightning back into its sheath, as a black kitten trotted through the branches sheltering her from the rain. It meowed eagerly when it saw her, its ratlike tail waving like a banner. Staggering over to Alanna, the tiny animal ordered her to pick him up.

The squire obeyed the kitten's command. Cuddling it against her shoulder, she searched her saddlebags for her blanket.

"How did you get here, little cat?" she asked, gently toweling it dry. "It's a bad night for *anyone* to be out-of-doors."

The kitten purred noisily, as if it agreed. *The poor thing is skin and bones—not someone's pet,* Alanna reflected. Wondering what its eyes looked like, she lifted its chin with a careful finger, and gulped. The black kitten's large eyes were as purple as her own.

"Great Merciful Mother," she breathed with reverence. Settling by the fire, she fed her guest as she thought. She had never heard of a *cat* with purple eyes. Was it supernatural? An immortal, perhaps? If so, she wasn't sure she wanted anything to do with it. She had troubles enough!

His stomach full, the small animal began to wash vigorously. Alanna laughed. Violet eyes didn't make a creature supernatural. Weren't she and Thom proof of that? This cat certainly behaved like a normal animal. Thinking of something, she lifted her new pet's tail and checked its sex. Satisfied he was a male, and ignoring his protests against the indignity, Alanna settled him on her lap. The kitten grumbled for a few moments, then settled himself. She leaned back against the willow's broad trunk, listening to the animal's very loud purr. *It'll be nice to have a pet to talk to,* she thought sleepily.

The sneezes hit her, five at once, blinding her momentarily. Swearing like a guardsman, Alanna wiped her watering eyes. When she could see, a tall hooded stranger was standing beside her fire!

Alanna jumped to her feet, her sword unsheathed and ready, spilling the yelling cat to the ground. She stared at the newcomer, fighting to calm herself. She had no right to attack this—man? woman?—simply because she had been surprised.

"May I be of service?" she gasped. The kitten was tugging on her boot, demanding to be held once more. "Hush," she told it before looking at the stranger again.

"I saw your fire through the trees." The newcomer's voice was husky and soft, like the wind blowing through the treetops, and yet somehow Alanna was reminded of a pack of hounds belling in the hunt. "Would you permit me to warm myself?"

Alanna hesitated, then nodded. The stranger threw back the concealing hood, revealing a woman—the tallest woman Alanna had ever seen. Her skin was perfectly white, setting off slanting emerald eyes and full red lips. Her hair was unbound, falling loosely below her shoulders in black, snaky locks. Alanna gulped. The woman's face was too perfect to be quite real, and she settled before the fire with boneless grace. She watched Alanna as she sat down clumsily again, her amazingly green eyes unreadable.

"It is odd to see a youngling alone in this place," she said at last. Her mouth curved in a tiny smile. "There are strange tales about this tree, and what passes beneath it."

The kitten jumped back into Alanna's lap and purred. Alanna stroked it nervously, never taking her eyes away from her visitor.

"I was caught by the storm," she answered carefully. "This was the first shelter I found." *And now I'm sorry I found it,* she added to herself. *I don't like surprises!*

The woman looked her over carefully, still smiling that hooded smile. "And so, my daughter, now you are a squire. Within four years you will be a knight. That doesn't seem so far from now, does it?"

Alanna opened and closed her mouth several times with surprise before biting her lips together. The "squire" part was easy; beneath her cloak she was wearing the royal uniform, as was required when squires went abroad without their masters. But the woman had called her "my daughter"; the stranger knew she was a girl, even though she was dressed as a boy with her breasts bound flat! And her own mother had died years ago, when Alanna was born. Suddenly she remembered that she had heard the woman's voice before. Where? At last she made the safest answer she could.

"I don't want to seem rude, but I'd rather not speak of the Ordeal," she said flatly. "I'd like not to *think* of it, if possible."

"But you must think of it, my daughter," the woman chided. Alanna frowned. She had almost remembered… "When you undergo the Ordeal of Knighthood, many things will happen. You will become a knight, the first woman knight in more than a hundred of your years. You will have to reveal your true sex soon after that; your own nature will not let you remain silent for long. I know well how much you hate living a lie before your friends at the palace."

Alanna stiffened. She had remembered that voice. Jonathan had been a boy, dying of the Sweating Sickness. The palace healers said there was no hope, but Alanna—only a page then—had gotten Sir Myles to convince them to let her use her healing Gift. The sorcery causing the fever was too much for the magic she knew, and in the end she had appealed to the Great Mother Goddess. She had heard a voice that hurt her ears—a woman's voice that sounded like a pack of hounds in full cry, like the huntress urging them on. And she had heard that voice again, only a year ago, when she and Jon were trapped in the Black City. They had called on the Goddess for help then, and she had told them what to do.

"That's impossible," she whispered, her voice shaking. "You—you can't be—"

"And why not?" the Mother asked. "It is time we talked, you and I. Surely you know that you are one of my Chosen. Is it so strange that I have come to you for a time, my daughter?"